The Adventures of
Bucket and Arthur

Moorland

Sheila E. Humphrey

2 4 6 8 10 9 7 5 3 1

sheilahumphrey62@gmail.com

ISBN 978-1-0698130-0-8

Cover Design and Interior Typesetting by
FOGLIO | CUSTOM BOOK SPECIALISTS
Body set in *Adobe Aldine VF*
Titles set in *Journal OT Text*

F O G L I O P R I N T . C O M

Actual events from the early 1990s propelled me to write *The Adventures of Bucket and Arthur.* I dedicate the series of six books to my children, Will and Melina. Their lives continue to delight, challenge and amaze.

Moorland

Chapter One

Survival Tactics

IT HAPPENED SO QUICKLY THAT ARTHUR WAS ON HIS BACK and in the dirt before he knew it. Henry and Greg glared down at him, shaking their fists in his face.

"And don't even think of coming in our part of the schoolyard ever again!" Greg yelled.

Arthur stayed down, catching his breath. By the time he got to his feet and brushed himself off, his two classmates were chasing after his best friend, Addison. But Arthur knew they might have some trouble catching him. Addison was a first-rate soccer player and could run like a jackrabbit, bobbing and weaving. He could change direction in a split second. Arthur watched with amusement as Addison swerved behind the baseball backdrop, causing Greg and Henry to collide with each other. Greg had anticipated the move, but Henry just wasn't as quick on his feet. The result—minor mayhem, while Addison glanced back and casually jogged clear of the intended punishment.

As they stood in line, waiting to go into the school, Arthur and Addison made their way to the front of the row, sneaking by under the noses of the lunchtime supervisors.

"Hey, good one Add!" Arthur whispered. "You sure had them going."

"Yeah. Maybe they need to watch less TV and get like, a little more exercise."

At the back of the line, out of breath, Henry and Greg jostled each other as they filed into the school. They hadn't gotten Addison this time. Their frustration at their lack of success seemed to spill over at one another.

"You stupid idiot," Greg declared. "Couldn't you see where Add was going?"

"Aw, c'mon Greg," Henry whined. "It was your idea. We never get him that way. You know we can't."

"Geez, idiot. I'm always the only one with ideas! Let me know when the light bulb goes on in *your* head OK?"

They were still shoving each other when they got to their classroom. Miss Mitchell, their third grade teacher, saw them fighting and assumed a quarrel was in progress. She made them sit with their heads down for five minutes for an "official time out".

The rest of the class quietly opened their books and read silently for the requisite fifteen minutes of DEAR—Drop Everything and Read. It was another one of Miss Mitchell's innovations. After three years of teaching, she had discovered that it was one of the best techniques for getting a class to simmer down after a hectic lunch recess. It wasn't foolproof—what was? But at least it gave her students time to re-focus, relax a bit, and get their brains re-oriented. It also gave her time to catch her breath and think about the afternoon's flow of events. Sometimes she would walk around and ask children questions about the books they were reading, or just make a mental note which students were into chapter books and which ones were idly paging through a book just to look at the pictures.

Arthur, meanwhile, was enjoying the book he had checked out from the Moorland Public Library. It was about UFOs, a subject Arthur was very curious about. His fascination with the subject had started with something his sister, Bucket, had talked about at supper one evening. She claimed that their great uncle Ken had actually seen seven UFOs flying in formation. Arthur couldn't believe such a ridiculous statement, but then their mother confirmed it! After that he devoured anything and everything he could read about the subject.

Addison was looking at an illustrated underwater encyclopedia. Ever since his father had taken his family snorkelling at Cabo San Lucas, he had been fascinated by the brilliantly-coloured, tropical fish. He was looking forward to the day when he would be old enough to go deep sea diving, and really see some bigger creatures. As he turned a page in his book, a vivid photograph of a hammerhead shark caught his attention.

"Hmmm. That one, kinda looks like Greg," he thought, chuckling. Seymour looked up startled and made him realize he had chuckled out loud.

Addison tilted the big book so Seymour could see what he was looking at. Seymour nodded, smiled in approval and mouthed the word, "wow".

The rest of the afternoon disappeared quickly in a kaleidoscope of seatwork: note-copying in health, math problem solving, and a pop quiz in social studies.

Addison dawdled after school, suspecting that his tormentors would be waiting for him. When he asked if he could stay a while and help clean up, Miss Mitchell welcomed his help.

"After you've erased the board, would you mind tidying up the library?"

"Um, sure Miss Mitchell."

"You walk to school, don't you?"

"Yes, Miss Mitchell." Addison glanced out the window. He could see Greg on the playground, shaking his fist at him.

"Are you sure this is alright with your mother, to stay after school?"

"Oh yes, Miss Mitchell!" Addison exclaimed.

Miss Mitchell pulled back from what seemed like a useless line of inquiry. She thought that it was wonderful for any student to express an interest in staying after school, but Addison was not particularly forthcoming in any of his responses. It was difficult at best, really, to get any response out of him.

Lately she had noticed that Addison liked to stay after school more frequently. Well, she wasn't going to question any child's enthusiasm for helping out in the classroom. Perhaps, when she had a moment, a quick call to his mom might be in order. His mother could be thinking that she had actually required Addison to stay in, for whatever reason.

Chapter Two

Tuning In

OUT ON THE PLAYGROUND, Greg's mother had already picked him up for hockey practice. Arthur was relieved that he had successfully avoided Greg and Henry that afternoon by hiding in the boy's washroom. He knew that without Greg, Henry wouldn't do anything, except maybe taunt him.

All this time, Bucket had been circling the school looking for her brother.

"Hey, Arthur! Hurry up," she called from the across the playground, when she saw him coming out of the school.

"OK. Wait for me", he yelled. Arthur hurried along, grabbing his UFO book and stuffing it in his backpack. He had been reading in the washroom, standing up on a toilet seat to avoid detection.

"I was beginning to worry," Bucket said.

"Hey don't worry about me. I can take care of myself!"

"Not saying you can't, bro. But we've got to move if we're going to get to choir in time."

"Hey, someone told me you tried out for the school musical," Arthur said, changing the subject.

"Yeah, well, we'll see what happens." Bucket gave Arthur a rueful smile as they walked along the sidewalk away from the school. "Me and the whole fifth grade class tried out. It'll just be for fun, no matter who gets what, right?"

"Sure Bucket. I know you'll have fun. But I bet you're a shoo-in for a big part."

"Well, Miss Cauldwell is very particular. Each of us had to sing 'Happy Birthday'. And she took notes. You know what? That's not the easiest song to sing by yourself!"

"Aw c'mon, Bucket. You know three verses, remember?"

So as Bucket and Arthur walked along, they sang the three verses to 'Happy Birthday'. Arthur's voice hadn't changed yet, and his high soprano notes matched Bucket's. Sometimes he sang the higher part just to tease her. As they sang they scarcely noticed a distinct chill in the air that came with early spring.

Arthur's backpack was showing signs of high use. His mother had done a recent patching job, but every day it seemed there was a new seam coming undone. The straps especially had been re-sewn a few times. Bucket's answer to backpack repair was to use duct-tape. At this time of year at least a portion of her pack was covered with the silver mending tape. She had embellished this with permanent marker to create a colourful swirling design. Bucket explained to her skeptical mother that it was an ongoing art project.

Arthur and Bucket went to school and to choir in the old part of town. Their city, Moorland, was big and only getting bigger. It was so big that each section of the city seemed like its own town. The old part had lots of churches, corner stores, and schools. Everyone walked or bicycled because it wasn't too hilly, and you didn't really need your car to go to the neighbourhood store only two blocks away.

The street they were walking down was lined with big American elm trees. Their graceful, dark branches formed an archway over the narrow street. The brick church on the corner was the choir's venue. A giant Mayday tree grew in the front beside the wide steps that led to the double glass doors.

Mrs. Black, the choir's manager, greeted them as they entered. Her hair, a white blonde, was always perfectly in place, and her smile was warm and welcoming.

"Bucket and Arthur! I think they've just started rehearsal. Come see me at break for the newsletter. Don't forget!" she said.

The siblings clattered down the stairs to the basement of the old church. In the big meeting hall, chairs were set up in a semi-circle facing the conductor, Ms. Moster. Bucket proceeded to sit between her two friends Rowena and Pro (short for Providence), while Arthur took his appointed spot next to his buddy Lance.

Ms. Moster, who had been going through the important points of the newsletter, was saying,

"—So next year is our tour year. We will be going to England, Scotland, and Wales. It's really important that we get some indication of the interest in the choir before the summer holidays. Now, I know it's even before our spring concert, but it doesn't hurt to talk to your moms and dads about it now!"

Immediately a buzz went up among the choir. Everyone started talking at once, excitedly going over the possibilities of travel to somewhere so far away.

"All right, everyone! Let's put the newsletters away. We have a concert to prepare for, and we don't have much time. You can talk about this at break."

"Shhh, you guys," Bucket whispered to her two friends. Ms. Moster was so nice. Bucket always got annoyed when the choir wouldn't listen to her. Mrs. Cauldwell, her music teacher from school, was so different, but then she was a lot older and bigger than Ms. Moster.

After an hour of rehearsal, Bucket headed off with her friends to get their snacks and talk on their break. Arthur, with Lance in the lead, went to find Mrs. Black.

"Hey, Mrs. Black!" Lance yelled when they reached the church foyer. "You got any more of those newsletters? Me and my buddy here didn't get one."

"Well, if it isn't Mr. Sabre! How did you sneak in this time?" Mrs. Black asked. "I can't mark you present if I don't see you. And your mom and dad would be asking me where you are and I wouldn't be able to tell them!"

"Aw, I can't give away all my secrets. Anyway, it's Arthur's fault. He's the one who always gets me into trouble," Lance said.

"Did not," Arthur exclaimed, though with half a smile.

"Did too," Lance said, jabbing him in the ribs.

"OK. That's enough, *gentlemen*," Mrs. Black admonished. "Just see that these newsletters get to your parents. And Arthur, I'm only giving you one for both you and Bucket. Make sure you bring me that back page signed next week."

"Yes, Mrs. Black," Arthur said, taking the newsletter and stuffing it in his back pocket.

"Aye, aye, Mrs. Black," stated Lance, giving her a salute and clicking his heels together. "We will accept this dangerous mission!"

"Oh, get on with you," Mrs. Black said, laughing and swatting them with her hand as they clambered down the stairs to the basement.

Bucket met them as they entered the rehearsal room.

"Did you get the newsletter?" she asked Arthur, when she didn't see anything in his hands.

"Oh yeah, it's here," said Arthur, pulling out a now-crumpled sheaf of papers.

"Right, I'll just take that over, OK.?" Bucket said, as she took them from her brother and patiently smoothed out the wrinkled pages.

"Boy, you're lucky to have a sister to organize you," Lance stated.

"Oh yeah, you don't know the half of it!" Arthur exclaimed, rolling his eyes. But then he caught Bucket's eye as she turned to go, and he gave her a wink.

The choir was still talking when Ms. Moster rapped her baton on the music stand. Carey Biggs, the accompanist, played a few chords from Grieg's "In the Hall of the Mountain King," and the choir slowly quieted down.

Carey was a lot of fun, and he always enjoyed getting their attention by playing a variety of selections from his repertoire, although, sometimes he extended his performance time right into the rehearsal. Ms. Moster was usually extremely patient, and seemed to enjoy his musicality as much as the choir. However, today she said,

"Mr. Biggs, could we have the introduction to "The Streets of London"—*please?*"

Total silence fell over the choristers. Ms. Moster rarely raised her voice, and when she did it was never at Mr. Biggs. It was a side to their director that most of the choir had never seen before.

"Choir, you know that Mrs. Cauldwell will be coming next week to work with you. Let's at least be knowledgeable of the music, before she gets here. I don't mean that it has to be performance standard, but it needs to be a little better than sight-reading!"

Lance's hand shot up.

"Can't this wait?" Ms. Moster asked.

"Well, I just wanted to know—will she be as mean to us here as she is at school?" Lance asked, looking around to see what effect his daring question had on those around him.

"Lance, that is really an uncalled for question. Mrs. Cauldwell was the director of this choir before you were born! We have only to be grateful that she still wants to help us and be involved with the organization. We're really very, very lucky." And for good measure, Ms. Moster glared at the rest of the children, daring anyone to disagree. The group was much more subdued when they got out their music folders and prepared to sing again.

After choir, sitting on the church steps while waiting for their mom, Bucket and Arthur discussed the details of the rehearsal. Everyone else had gone home, except Mrs. Black. She was inside the church, tidying up and organizing the music for next week's practices. Their mother was leading a workshop somewhere and was going to be a little late.

"Are you going to try out for any of the solo parts?" Arthur asked his sister.

"I'm not sure. That's something for the teens in the choir. Besides, I'm not that good," Bucket answered, while putting down her music folder and backpack.

"Aw c'mon Bucket. You tried out for the musical. What's the

difference?" Arthur couldn't understand his sister's reluctance.

"Like, um, in school there aren't that many singers. In choir, well, everyone sings," she said.

"Besides, *you* should try out. You have a higher voice than me, something you're always bugging me about." She gave Arthur a friendly shove.

"Yeah. And you're going to be the only one that ever knows. It would be worse than dweeb city if that ever got out." He hung his head.

"Don't worry. You're secret's safe with me." Bucket gave him a hug. Then trying to lighten the atmosphere, she asked,

"Hey, what do you think about the tour?"

She pulled the choir's newsletter from her choir folder. They read over the details, noting the different cities and festivals that they would be attending if they were able to go. By the time their mother drove up they were both excited and eager to discuss the possibility with her.

Chapter Three

Home Time

She drove up in their old Toyota gold hatchback. Their mom called it "mellow yellow," not old or gold. She had bought it when it was ten years old already, which was now a few years ago. Hurrying out of the car, she gave each of the children a hug before they climbed in. She ran up the church steps two at a time and was breathless when she opened the door..

"I'm so sorry, Mrs. Black. Thanks so much for hanging around with the kids. I really hate it when they schedule my workshops on choir day. It's just insane!" she said. Mrs. Black had her coat on and was getting out her keys.

"Think no more of it, Florence," she said as she ushered Bucket and Arthur's mother out the door. "You know that they're no trouble. Besides, I had sorting to do and I got it all done!"

"You don't know how relieved I am, Diane. Thanks again!" Florence sprinted back down the steps to the waiting car.

"Oh, there's a newsletter for you too, Flo. I'm not sure which one of them has it," Mrs. Black said. Laughing, she waved and walked away.

All the way home, Bucket and Arthur talked about the choir

tour to the United Kingdom. They were so excited that they didn't notice their mother's silence on the subject.

The streets were dappled gold in the light of an early spring evening. The hedge on their corner lot was starting to show brown bud casings. The peony on the house's east side was emerging from the cold earth. As they walked from the garage to the house, laden down with their packs, bags and folders, they could see Presto's black face in the kitchen window. A black bearded-collie mix, she had a hairy, slightly wild looking muzzle.

"We're coming, Presto!" Arthur called, running up the back porch steps.

"Arthur, can you take Presto for a walk while I make dinner?" their mother asked as she opened the door to their home. Presto attacked them as they entered, jumping up on each one and barking enthusiastically.

Bucket bent down and petted the dog.

"Yes, we're home now, Presto. It's OK. What a good dog." She continued to calm the dog, talking and getting her to sit down. Presto's tail still wagged furiously, especially when she saw Arthur bring the leash.

"Now, Arthur, don't go into the park, it's too dark. Just go up and down the block a few times. You know how she loves to sniff everything anyway. We'll get her out for a good run tomorrow," instructed his mother.

"Do you need any help Mom?" Bucket asked as she opened the door for Arthur and Presto.

"No, you go ahead and do your homework. This is my therapy—culinary therapy," her mother explained as she hung up their coats and plunked her briefcase on a dining room chair. She rolled up her sleeves, opened the refrigerator door, and started to place food on the adjacent counter.

It was a very small kitchen. The sink was on a short wall between the hall door, which led to the bedrooms and living room, and the door to the basement and back porch. The oven and refrigerator rested side by side. A nook with a window housed a small counter with cupboards over top and underneath. This was the multi-purpose counter because it was the only counter available. On either side of the sink was just enough counter space to hold dirty and clean dishes. In order to open the oven door, it was necessary to back down the stairs leading to the basement and back porch.

But the kitchen had a certain charm about it. The backsplash above the sink was done in earthy tones, which warmed up the white cupboards and appliances. It was too small a kitchen for a dishwasher or even a microwave. Nevertheless, they had managed to host turkey dinners and other celebratory events in the last few years.

The house was almost fifty years old. The refrigerator was a 1954 model and had its own butter regulator. Florence thought that it must have been top of the line in its day. However, finding replacement parts was impossible, so she knew that it was only a matter of time before it would have be replaced.

The basement was once used as someone's apartment. The kitchen downstairs was actually bigger than the one on the main floor, but it just didn't have the same personality. It was the old-style counter top with chrome edging, and felt cold and cheerless. The living room was great for a children's play area, and there was an extra bedroom for guests. Florence didn't have the money to fix it up. She had spent it all when they had moved in. She bought some new casement windows for the top floor and re-did the hardwood floors. There was also a beautiful Petrof piano sitting in the living room.

The downstairs refrigerator was perfect when there was company. Florence could put all the drinks and extra food items in there and not worry about having enough room in the upstairs fridge.

In a little while the smells of spaghetti sauce filled the air. The pasta pot quietly bubbled its contents. Bucket and her mother were setting the table, as Arthur came in the door with the dog. Presto was panting heavily and really smelled of damp dog.

"Wow, you gave her a run anyway, Arthur," his mother commented.

"It started to rain, Mom. I decided to run with Presto. She loved it!" Arthur said as he shrugged out of his wet jacket.

"Get that towel rag from under the kitchen sink. She needs drying, that's for sure! Don't forget her feet."

At dinner, talk was all about Bucket's audition for the school musical and the upcoming choir tour. Arthur was mainly interested in exploring the mysteries of Stonehenge, while Bucket really liked the idea of seeing London and Trafalgar Square.

Finally their mother said, "actually, I think I might have some news too. I've been awarded a sabbatical for next year," she proudly stated and looked at each of her children.

"Uh, mom, what's a sabbatical?" Arthur wondered.

"It's a year when your mother gets paid to go to school and *not* to go to work. The official approval just came through today. That was one of the reasons I was so late picking you up from choir. I didn't find out until after the workshop was over. Well, isn't that great?!" she asked, looking from one to the other.

"You mean you *want* to go to school?" Arthur asked, incredulous.

"Of course, Arthur, it's like an honour. Isn't it, mom?" Bucket said, trying to explain.

"Yes, it is. There sure aren't many sabbaticals given, and it was a huge surprise for me! I have to promise to come back right afterwards. It's only for a year, and it has to be for next year. It will mean a cut in pay, but I'll figure that out. I'm sure that it will work out, somehow. OK, seriously, what do you think?"

"Mom, that is so cool. I'm really proud of you!" Bucket said, getting up and giving her mother a big hug.

"Sure mom," said Arthur, getting up and giving his mother a big hug so he wouldn't be outdone by his sister. Presto, who had taken up an advantageous position under the table, eagerly jumped up and wagged her tail.

"Look, mom," Bucket said. "Presto's congratulating you too!"

Chapter Four
Gabriel and Gwyneth—Part I

LATER THAT NIGHT, FLORENCE KNOCKED on Arthur's door and entered. He was lying on his bed, with a sketch pad and pencil. She sat on his desk chair and asked,

"What are you writing, Arthur?" Once, when Arthur was two years old Florence had called him Art, but it just didn't seem to fit. After that she had always called him Arthur, and so had everybody else. She smoothed his wispy blond hair off his forehead.

"Stuff." Arthur said looking at her. "It's just stuff."

"Are you in a sharing mood?" his mother asked.

"Not finished yet." He sat up and closed the sketch book.

Arthur's mother picked up his backpack and asked,

"Is there anything I should be seeing in here? Did you finish your homework?" She heaved the pack up onto her knees, and noticed a freshly ripped seam.

"I guess so," Arthur replied. "Here's my agenda, mom." He passed her the dog-eared, coil-bound book. She turned to the appropriate date and noted Arthur's shorthand in pencil. He always printed, even though his cursive writing was actually quite legible. His printing tended to run together and appear as one long word.

Florence considered that teachers were usually very good at getting to know each of their student's writing idiosyncrasies. She was definitely good at deciphering all of her own students. After so many years, she had practice. Arthur simply could not be persuaded to write in cursive, even though his work was so much easier to understand that way. There were only so many battles in life that were worth fighting, and Florence had determined that this was not one of them.

"I see you have a spelling test tomorrow. Do you want to go over any of these words?" she asked Arthur.

"OK, mom. I guess it won't take long," he said. Arthur sighed and laid back down on the bed, rolling over onto his back.

And so Florence went down the list, with Arthur spelling each word correctly, until they came to the word "people."

"Umm...p-e-e-p-e-l," Arthur tentatively spelled.

"Well, I guess that *is* the way the word sounds. With this word, you might have to make it sound differently in order to get it right. Try saying pee-opp- ell-ee—and that's the way that it's spelled...p-e-o-p-l-e—pee-opp-ell-ee. Now try it," his Mother coaxed.

"All right, mom," Arthur said, pausing for effect and clearing his throat. "I...t..." He pronounced clearly.

"What?"

"Yup," Arthur smiled. "You said, 'Now try *it*'!" Arthur laughed and looked to his mother.

"Why, you rascal," Florence exclaimed as she promptly hit him with the agenda and then started to tickle him, dumping the backpack on the floor. Arthur shrieked with laughter. He was never able to withstand a good tickle.

Bucket appeared at the door with Presto at her heels. Seeing that they were having such a good time, she decided to join in the fray. Pretty soon all three were tickle attacking each other and calling out who should be the next target, with Presto barking encouragement. Finally, panting and dishevelled, they stopped and sat up one by one.

"What was going on, you guys?" Bucket asked.

"Mom was giving me a spelling test," declared Arthur, and he laughed again.

"I wish my spelling tests were that hilarious," Bucket said. "Mine are twenty-five words long every week. And I just suck at spelling!"

"Bucket! I've told you not to use that word. It's kind of rude. I mean, are you alluding to a suckling pig, for example?"

"Mom, what's alluding mean?" asked Bucket. She was always questioning her Mother's vocabulary. Sometimes she did it to understand what her mother was saying and, at other times it was because she wanted to try the word herself. It helped that her teacher, Mr. Harbicht, tried to encourage her classmates to bring new words for the classroom's word wall every month.

"It means 'to refer to' something. When you are alluding to something, you don't say what you mean to say outright. For example, if I say, 'Oh my goodness, look at the time, Arthur.' I could be alluding to the fact that it's Arthur's bedtime without really coming out and saying it."

"Is that a subtle hint, Mom?" Arthur asked innocently.

"You're so perceptive, Arthur!" their mother said.

"Mom, what's perceptive mean?" asked Bucket.

"No, no stop! Not again! I'm going to dieeeeee!" Arthur wailed.

"Actually, mom," Bucket said, getting that I-know-you're-really-going-to-want-to-do-this look in her eye, "I thought you might like to tell us a G-G story." Then she flashed her mother a winning smile.

"Yes, Mom," Arthur reinforced, "we haven't heard one for ages!"

"Are you sure you're not just avoiding your bedtime?" their mother said, looking at them both sternly.

"Of course not!" they both chimed in unison.

"We really haven't done storytelling for a while—Hmmm...," their mother said, looking thoughtful. "Didn't you always ask me for certain beginnings and endings?"

"OK. How about sad at the beginning, crazy in the middle, and then..." Bucket paused.

"—And then happy in the end," Arthur finished.

"Yikes," their Mother said, but she smiled. The whole family settled in, finding comfortable spots. Florence sat in the desk chair and put her feet up on Arthur's backpack. Bucket and Arthur lay on the small bed, each finding a pillow to scrunch up and making room for Presto, who seemed to like stories too. They both looked at their mother expectantly.

"Well, you know that Gabriel and Gwyneth lived in a little house next to the woods. Their house was the last one on the last street in that part of town. In front of their house was the very last street light. It cast a golden glow in the early dusk of winter. Yes, it was winter. In fact, on this particular night, the snow was softly falling.

"Gwyneth was out in the side yard, gathering up a load of wood for the fireplace, while Gabriel was sweeping out the back porch. Their mother was finishing up in the kitchen, drying the dishes. Gwyneth stomped up

the steps to the porch and tapped on the door with her foot.

"'Hey, open up! My hands are full!' she yelled. Since Gabriel was sweeping up the last of the dirt with the dustpan, Gwyneth was left holding her load of wood for a few minutes. Suddenly she froze, becoming perfectly still. She had heard a very strange sound.

"'Hurry up in there. Hurry up!' Gwyneth cried, getting quite scared at that point. She hit the door again and again with her foot.

"'What's all the fuss?' her mother asked as she opened the door with Gabriel beside her. Gwyneth barged in, stomping snow off her feet and throwing the cut logs into the wood box they kept on the back porch.

"'Hey, I just cleaned up in here!' groused Gabriel.

"'Sorry, but I heard a really strange noise out there. And you know how dark it is! I don't know...maybe I just imagined it.'

"'Oh Gwyneth, I'm sure it's nothing. Gabriel and I will get our coats on and we'll go outside to listen and look,' their mother said.

"So they bundled up, put on their boots, and grabbed a flashlight. Gabriel led the way out to their backyard. Their mother held up her hand and said,

"'OK. Let's just listen.' So they huddled together and looked out into the darkness. They waited and waited. The only sound was their own breath, which they could see in the cold, still air. And then suddenly Gabriel passed gas.

"'C'mon Gabriel!' moaned his sister, 'what did you do that for?'

"'Hey, it wasn't me: it must've been you!' he replied. And then they all started laughing. They turned to go back inside, walking slowly, but then they heard a faint crying sound. It riveted them to the spot. And then they heard it again.

"'I think it's coming from the woods. Let's see if we can follow the

sound,' their mother said as she turned on the flashlight and motioned them to follow.

"The footpath into the woods bordered their back fence and then branched out into two different directions. Tonight, because of the falling snow, they were making the first footprints. When they came to the fork in the road, they all stopped to listen.

"'Mom, I think it's coming from the right,' Bucket whispered after they heard the sound again. They walked a few tentative steps in that direction and then stopped again. Sure enough, a type of desperate crying could be heard—this time a little louder.

"'All right, let's keep going. Stay close,' whispered their mother. The trees of the woods rose up beside them as they shuffled slowly along. The snow was falling thicker, so the air seemed dappled with light. The flashlight created a flickering beam ahead of them as it illuminated the snowflakes.

"'Over here!' Gabriel cried out. 'I think I see something. The sound's coming from this sack on the ground!' They hurried to where Gabriel crouched, the flashlight's beam jerking around as they found their way to the snowy bundle nestled deep within a copse of trees.

"'It's moving!' Gwyneth exclaimed."

Florence yawned and said, "Well, I guess we should stop the story here for tonight."

"You must be joking!" Arthur complained.

"Yeah mom, you can't stop at the most exciting part of the story!" Bucket sat up and tossed her pillow at her mother. Florence just chuckled as she caught it.

"Tomorrow's a working day for all of us. And, hey, it gives me more time to think up what comes next!" Florence got out of the chair and threw the pillow back at Bucket. Presto leapt off the bed and jumped up on Florence.

"Just you wait and see...ha, ha, ha, ha!" she sang as she exited the room with the dog. "Lights out in fifteen minutes, everyone."

Chapter Five

The Winds of Change

THAT NIGHT, FLORENCE QUIETLY TIDIED UP in the living room after the children were asleep. She was by no means a neat freak, but she at least wanted to be able to navigate the house without stepping on something that might require her to get stitches. When the children were toddlers they were blessed with a great number of toys from friends and relatives. She used to regularly pack up a select number of toys to disappear and retrieve them after an interval had passed. The kids always reacted to these changes with delight, and watching their process of rediscovery was fun for Florence too.

The dog was on Bucket's bed when Florence went to check on them. Presto would then jump up on Arthur's bed part way through the night, eventually ending up on her own bed in the morning. Presto had always done this. When the family went on walks together, Presto would constantly run from one person to another, making sure the last one in the line kept up with the others. Florence surmised that it was the herding instinct that was a part of the dog's pedigree—if a mutt had a pedigree, that is.

Presto had been in the family since Arthur was a just a toddler. Her ex-husband's writer friend had a very hairy bearded collie that had never been spayed. The story was that the beagle from down the street had gotten loose in the alley and found the gate to the author's backyard open. The result was a litter of six adorable puppies, some black and some mottled black and brown. Presto was the liveliest and the smallest of the six. The little puppy had come right up to Bucket when they went to see the animals. Bucket was also the one who had named the puppy. Presto was one of the musical terms she had learned in choir, and seeing the puppy move so quickly, the name stuck.

When they brought Presto home, Arthur was only a year old, although he had started to walk at eleven months. When Presto was a puppy, she loved to jump up on Arthur in a spirit of play. Arthur would topple over, but he would pick himself up, laughing, and never complain.

In all the upheaval in their lives five years ago, the dog had remained one of the constants in their lives. She had mellowed a bit since she was a puppy, but Presto was still eager to play with Bucket and Arthur and run when they went for walks. They were lucky to live near a park where they could let Presto off the leash. She came when she was called, but she had never mastered the art of heeling. Her long black fur would sometimes become matted if left unattended, and even her paws looked feathered. As a very hairy companion, she was warm to snuggle up to.

The phone rang. Florence, who was at the dining room table in the middle of doing her paper work, reluctantly rose to get it.

"Hi, Florence," said a clear, strong voice. It was her sister, calling long distance from Saskatchewan.

"Hi, Edie," Florence said. "I was going to call you. I have news".

"I've got something to tell you too!" Edie exclaimed.

"You go first," Florence said. Edie was her big sister.

"We're coming for Easter this year! Wilt was able to get his assistant manager to work for that week, so we'll finally get to take a break. What do you think?" Edie asked.

"It should be good. I think Jean has the kids for part of the week-end, but we can work something out, I'm sure," Florence responded.

"Well, he'd better work something out!" Edie affirmed. She had never taken to Jean and all his assorted relatives, and she was even less enamoured with the group since Florence and Jean had divorced.

"Oh, Edie. It will be all right. You know we try to be flexible," Florence said, attempting to tone down Edie's strident reaction.

She and Jean had been divorced for almost three years, and before that, separated for two. Florence had resigned herself to being single, finding a satisfying life through work and her children. She went out of her way to facilitate times between her children and her ex's family. It only made sense to her that they have a good relationship. Bucket and Arthur were called by her ex-husband's last name, while Florence had reverted to her maiden name of Dunne. She reasoned that if they were happy together, then her kids would not feel cheated from having a normal family life. Fun times with their father and their mother, although not all at once, at least achieved some kind of normalcy. It was extremely important to Florence that her children not be short-changed in life.

"Yes, that's wonderful Florence—but it certainly strikes me that you're the one who's always being flexible!" Edie retorted.

"I just don't want them to miss out. Jean said he was going to take them fishing, and you know how much Arthur enjoys that," Florence said.

"Right! Jean gets to be the papa to all his children. I bet he enjoys that!" snorted Edie.

"I think I know what you mean. It was really difficult to get him to do things with the kids before the divorce. Now, it's quite amusing to see him make all of the social arrangements and include them in his new family," Florence said ruefully.

"Imagine, becoming a father again at his age," laughed Edie. "We can safely say that there is poetic justice in the real world."

"I certainly agree with you there, Edie. Remember what Mom used to say—there's no fool--"

"—like an old fool," Edie chimed in.

"But you know that Bucket especially loves that little baby. She is her sister, well, her half-sister—and I think they can grow up to at least be friends. Don't you think?" asked Florence.

"I don't know about you, Flo. You're the eternal optimist as far as I'm concerned. It'll be what it'll be. I really don't know how you can forgive that creep and his family for what you had to go through," Edie said, getting indignant again.

"It's called 'moving on,' Edie, and I have to do it or I'll get all bitter and twisted. And you don't want your sister all scrunched up and mean and ugly...Ha, ha, ha, ha, ha," cackled Florence, ending in a wicked witch crescendo of evil laughter. On the other line, Edie was laughing too.

"OK, OK. I'll let you keep your rose-coloured glasses. But I thought you said you had news?"

"Are you ready? My sabbatical came through!" Florence said with evident excitement. "It's for a whole year, all of next year. I really couldn't believe it. I just found out after my workshop tonight."

"That is amazing, Flo! What did the children say?" asked Edie.

"Actually, they said they were proud of me, but Arthur couldn't understand why I'd voluntarily want to go back to school," chuckled Florence.

"But it will be such a wonderful opportunity. Where are you going to go?" Edie inquired.

"It's possible that I'll be able to start a master's program right here in town," Florence said. "It's early days yet, but you can be sure I'll be making lots of inquiries in the next little while. I can hardly wait."

"This just might change your life around, Flo."

"Hey! There's nothing wrong with my life right now!"

"I mean, you might meet some new faces. And you'll get out into the real world," Edie said, trying to explain her point of view.

"Hey! What's so unreal about my world, Edith?" Florence countered. She occasionally used her sister's full name when she really wanted to tease her.

"You know what I mean. All you do is work and look after the kids. Next year, you'll really be able to broaden your horizons. What about a university out of town? Then I could come and visit you there!" Edie cried, who was suddenly full of enthusiasm at the prospect of travel.

"Settle down, sis!" Florence exclaimed. "I've got to try the local university first, because it'll be so much cheaper. But I have already looked into Anna Sexton's university in Tirovica. Remember, she was the one who came to do those in-services last year? She was brilliant, and she's written some good books too! But for the sake of Bucket and Arthur, I'm applying to Moorland's university first," she said with conviction that she didn't really feel.

A former colleague of hers was a professor now at Moorland university and had been very encouraging. It could be that there was an opportunity for Florence to get into the local graduate school. It would certainly make her family's life simpler. The entrance requirements for the master's education program were notoriously tough, however. Florence rated her chances slim to nil, even with the support of her former associate.

"Well good for you. Mom would sure be proud of you," Edie said. Their mother had died fifteen years before and had never known any of her grandchildren. But that didn't stop Edie and Flo from thinking about her every time they talked.

"I hope she would be," Florence said quietly. "You know Edie, that hoya plant she gave me started to bloom this week. It's as if Mom knew something good was going to happen. Is it crazy to think that?" she wondered.

"I don't think so. Besides, you're crazy in a good way."

"Gee, thanks. At any rate, I'll keep you posted about what's going on...the continuing saga of the Dunne household of Moorland. Now, does that sound like a best seller or what?" chortled Florence.

"Don't shortchange yourself. You never know what the future brings, Florence. Anyway, the immediate future is for Easter. Wilt and I are both coming, so pencil us in," Edie stated.

"You bet. I'll put it on the calendar right now. It's a red-letter day when Wilt gets away," Florence added.

"Don't I know it? Well, good night, Flo, and congratulations."

"Thanks. Love you, sis."

"Love you too." And with that, Florence hung up the phone, smiling

Chapter Six

Warning Signs

A FEW HOURS LATER, RUBBING HER EYES WITH FATIGUE, Florence checked the door locks and looked in on Bucket. Presto was still on Bucket's bed. She was lying crosswise at the bottom, while Bucket had one foot out of the covers to accommodate her. Florence bent down and kissed Bucket's head, smoothing the hair off of her cheek and out of her eyes. Presto raised her head to acknowledge Florence, who patted her back. Then Presto closed her eyes and seemed to sink back into sleep.

Bucket's room faced the street. The light filtered through the slats of the horizontal wooden blinds revealing the neatness of her daughter's bedroom. Her desk had little piles of paper that were organized according to her different homework projects. Mr. Harbicht, the fifth grade teacher, had been instrumental in changing Bucket's work habits. Bucket had always had to work hard for her grades, but it was this year's teacher whose mandate was to foster good study habits too.

And although Bucket was a terrible speller, bit by bit even that was improving. Florence's good friend Jan Clayton, and her sister Dorothy were partly responsible for that. Every other week they tutored Bucket in language arts. They called Bucket the "happy scholar" and seemed to have great fun in thinking up new ways to facilitate Bucket's errant spelling. Bucket was actually a very creative storyteller, but teachers had always been blind to this ability because of her poor spelling. Bucket had certainly lucked out this year, with a cracker-jack teacher and good tutors to help her.

As Florence moved into Arthur's room, she pondered the differences between her two children. Arthur's teacher was just not as seasoned as Mr. Harbicht, but she did have some interesting ideas. Florence reasoned that there was also a big difference between the two classes. Miss Mitchell definitely had her hands full with a high proportion of boys, while the fifth grade teacher had only six boys in his classroom.

Jan and Dorothy weren't coaching Arthur yet. Surely the third grade wasn't one to get too worried about, even though Florence had some concerns. Arthur was a thinker and a wonderer, and his room reflected this abstract attitude. But this year, Arthur was even less focused than he had been. His backpack was on the floor, its contents spilling out. His desk was piled with books and papers and an odd sock, all helter-skelter. His sketch book was on the topmost pile. Florence carefully picked it up. She bent down, kissed Arthur on the forehead and quietly tiptoed out of his room, closing the door softly behind her.

Florence went into her own bedroom and switched on the bedside light. She sat on her bed and read the last entry in Arthur's sketch book:

Rain is falling. It falls and falls.

The dog is happy and runs in the puddles.
The rain falls and falls right into my mind.
I am the rain. And I am the puddle.

Under the printing was a pencil drawing. It was a series of concentric circles, each circle getting progressively darker, until the centre was pencilled pitch black. Florence closed the book and clasped it to her chest. She bowed her head, closed her eyes, and thought about what his words might really mean. Maybe there was no hidden meaning at all. She thought it was a tremendously creative leap for Arthur to imagine himself as the rain. In his little poem, the dog was happy. But it didn't feel like the poet was. Florence resolved that she must talk to Arthur's teacher tomorrow, even if it was a Friday. Up to now Arthur hadn't said that anything was bothering him. Bucket had also not told her about any problems that Arthur was having at school. It was a mystery, but one that Florence was determined to solve. She tiptoed back into Arthur's room and replaced the book where she had found it.

The next day, the morning chaos went as usual. They let Presto into the backyard to do her business. Everyone pitched in to make the day's lunches while Florence quickly put breakfast on the table. In no time at all, they were out the door. Florence had just started the car when she realized that they had forgotten to bring Presto in from the backyard.

She leapt out of the car and ran up the front steps. The walk way was wet from the previous night's rain, so she kicked off her shoes before heading across the living room floor and through the kitchen to the back door. The dog leapt up against the screen door, and as she opened it, Presto burst through, and jumped up on her. Florence looked down at her beige jacket, which was now covered in dog prints.

"Oh no, Presto! Look what you did!" Florence quickly located the rag from under the kitchen sink to wipe off the dog's paws. She had a hard time keeping Presto quiet and still enough to do the job. Finally she whipped off her jacket and threw it downstairs in the direction of the washing machine and ran to the front hall closet for a different spring coat to wear. The choice wasn't too difficult because only her jean jacket was left. It would have to do.

Back in the car, Bucket and Arthur were talking about their upcoming choir tour again. Their chatter ceased as soon as they saw their mom.

"What happened, Mom?" asked Bucket. "What took you so long?"

"Let's just call it more fun and games in the Dunne household. Presto was so glad to see me that she jumped up and put her muddy paws on my jacket. Now hang onto your hats!" their mother said as she put the car into gear and sped off.

When they arrived at Bannister Elementary School, Florence said good-bye to Bucket but asked Arthur to stay in the car for a minute.

"Is everything OK at school, Arthur?" she asked.

"'Course, mom. It's Friday," Arthur said as he got out of the car. He turned to her before walking away. "We're going to the Clayton's tonight, right?" he added, with a smile.

"You bet your life we are," assured his mother. "We'll go there after I get home from work. Have a great day, honey," she called. Arthur turned and disappeared into the school. Florence should have felt reassured by her son's answers, but there was just something in the way he spoke and the way he moved that didn't sit right with her. Miss Mitchell was definitely going to get a call from her today.

Chapter Seven

Bucket's Class

INSIDE BANNISTER ELEMENTARY, Bucket hung up her coat inside her locker. Because the school was only for younger children, all the students in the fourth, fifth, and sixth grades were assigned lockers in a separate wing. The school also had separate exits for each wing. They were commonly referred to as the "big kids' doors" and the "little kids' doors". When a student progressed from the "little kids'" to the "big kids'" part of the school it was a big step up. Not only did the students use a different entrance and exit, they were also able to use the coveted lockers.

Students were allowed to decorate the insides of their lockers, as long as the decorations were within reason. Bucket's locker was in between her two best friends, Rowena and Providence, who also happened to be in the choir with her as well. The inside of Bucket's locker was filled with nature pictures she had cut out of her mother's magazines, as well as a few candid photographs of her family. Prominent among these was one of Presto taken in a park they had once visited. The dog's ears were flapping in the breeze and her tongue was hanging out. It looked like she was enjoying some sort of joke.

Rowena and Providence favoured movie stars and pop singers.

The insides of their locker doors were plastered with pictures of their favourites. Each girl belonged to different celebrity fan clubs. They spent some of their recess time exchanging photos of their latest heart-throbs. Bucket wasn't interested in being a fan of pop singers or movie stars, but she enjoyed listening to all the gossip that her friends seemed to know by being loyal fans. Bucket thought it was all the intrigue surrounding each personality that kept their fan bases growing.

"Hey Bucket, they might put up the musical cast list today!" Providence said excitedly.

"Do you really think so?" Bucket asked.

"Yeah, I heard Mr. Harbicht talking to Mrs. Cauldwell when they came out of the staff room," said Rowena. "I thought I heard her say—'and it was a difficult decision'". Rowena was always the first one to hear the latest gossip and then tell her friends about it. Bucket never knew where she got some of her information, but it had never been wrong.

Inside the classroom, everyone was sitting and reading while their student agendas were placed on top of each desk. Mr. Harbicht quietly circulated the room, checking each agenda: collecting notes from parents and overdue homework assignments. Bucket and her friends quickly sat and got out their books too. Bucket read her mother's magazine, *Harrowsmith*. She really liked the pictures of different homes in the countryside. There were always humorous articles as well. This month's issue had an article about a man who had taken his family to live in the country after being in the city for years and years. Because he was such a greenhorn, he was always getting into crazy situations that made Bucket smile. Both Rowena and Providence preferred their fan magazines. Mr. Harbicht didn't mind what the students brought to class, as long as they read something. He even allowed books on cartoons.

As the last bell rang, Mr. Bolen came on the intercom with his announcements for the day. He had a big voice that carried through the school.

"Good morning, one and all!" Mr. Bolen blared. "It rained last night, so the playground is muddy. Stay on the tarmac and the basketball courts at recess today. Let's make Mr. Gizo's job easy. If anyone tracks mud into the school, you'll have me to answer to, and you'll be spending your lunchtime as Mr. Gizo's personal helper. Now, let's stand and sing 'O Canada.'" Mr. Bolen loved music and insisted on a robust rendering of the national anthem. He didn't mind if it was sung off-key as long as it was loud and energetic. When they had school assemblies once a month, the students could count on Mr. Bolen to sing the loudest. After the anthem, Mr. Bolen came on again.

"I have an announcement here from Mrs. Cauldwell. The list for *Pirates of Penzance* will be put on the bulletin board by the music room at morning recess. To all those who received a part: please pick up your scripts from Mrs. Cauldwell before you leave from school today. Now, let's get cracking!"

Someone new coming into the school may have been alarmed by Mr. Bolen's big voice. However, after two years as principal, everybody knew that his bark was definitely worse than his bite. Bannister Elementary bordered on two different areas: Bannister Bay and Cornfield. Surrounding the school was the suburb known as Bannister Bay, while Cornfield lay just to the North. The more affluent area was Bannister Bay. Fewer students came from Cornfield, so they and their parents were always in the minority. Because of this, most of the PTA board members came from the Bannister Bay area. Mr. Bolen was skilled at working with both sets of parents.

In the fifth grade classroom, the students were working with partners on a mathematical probability problem. Yesterday they had kept a chart of the number of times a quarter landed on either heads or tails after twenty tosses. Today was more complicated. Today they were rolling dice to see how often each side of the dice turned up after fifty tosses. Bucket's partner was the new girl in the school, Chim. She was very quiet and shy, but that was OK with Bucket. She only had sympathy for someone coming new late in the year. At least Chim could be a part of the musical. Bucket could hardly wait to see Mrs. Cauldwell's list!

After math, everyone moved back into their rows for language arts. Mr. Harbicht walked over to the word wall. There were four neat columns of handwritten words so far. Mr. Harbicht insisted on handwriting. It was a point of honour to get your word on the word wall, so everybody worked hard at perfecting their handwriting skills, at least for language arts. With only a few weeks until spring break, the class needed at least a dozen more new words before they could have a pizza party. They could only earn the party if they had successfully found fifty brand-new words.

Each term Mr. Harbicht started a new word wall, and each time it had a different theme. This term the theme had been 'mystery'. Everyone had been excited about the theme, but it was a challenge to get to the fifty-word mark. Mr. Harbicht didn't allow any single-syllable words. He also had a record of the previous word lists so that there would be no duplication. That meant it got harder and harder to come up with new words as the year went on. Bucket really wondered how difficult it would be to come up with something new in May and June. She hoped her word would get on the wall this time.

"Well, class," said Mr. Harbicht. "Is there anyone out there who thinks they have a word good enough for our word wall?" A few students raised their hands.

"Yes, Donald, do you have a word that we've never had before?" Mr. Harbicht inquired.

"Sure, and it has a lot to do with mystery," said Donald proudly. "And there is more than one word! Sherlock Holmes. Can I count it for two words, Mr. Harbicht?"

"Actually, you might remember that you can't use proper nouns," the teacher said. Donald couldn't help himself, and he groaned aloud.

"However, an exception can be made since this name is a very important one for our theme. I will not say any more until you give us your sentence that you have composed for your words. Well?" Mr. Harbicht asked expectantly. Each entry for the word wall had to be accompanied by a sentence that was not a definition for the word. The sentence had to make the meaning of the word clear without defining it. This had been a difficult concept at the beginning of the year, but now everyone was eager to show their prowess.

Donald cleared his throat and picked up his binder. "Everyone knew that the most difficult murder cases could be solved by Sherlock Holmes." He looked up at Mr. Harbicht inquiringly. There was a pause. Donald held his breath.

"Not bad, Donald, not bad at all," said Mr. Harbicht. "Does anybody, besides Donald, know about Sherlock Holmes?" Chim put her hand half-way up. Mr. Harbicht noticed and immediately motioned for her to speak.

"I think he was a detective in a book. He was very smart. And his friend was a doctor," Chim said. She spoke in a soft voice. Bucket caught her eye and smiled.

"That's exactly right, Chim," Mr. Harbicht affirmed. Chim sat up taller and smiled briefly. Their teacher had a knack for making each student feel like they had something important to contribute. And Chim was new. She had only been in Canada for a few months and had come to the school just a few weeks ago. It was the most she had ever said at one time. Mr. Harbicht continued,

"Sherlock Holmes and his sidekick, Doctor Watson, solved many complex mysteries in Victorian England. They were characters in a series of books by Sir Arthur Conan Doyle. And actually, *Pirates of Penzance,* the musical this class will be involved in, was written and performed at the same time that Sir Arthur Conan Doyle was writing his very popular mysteries.

"Donald, you may put 'Sherlock Holmes' as one entry on our word wall, and add your sentence to the word wall binder on my desk. Now, is there anyone else who has a contribution? I thought that I saw other hands go up," he said, looking around the room. Bucket tentatively put up her hand.

"Ah, Miss Boisvert, what have you got for us today?" Mr. Harbicht asked with a slight smile on his lips.

"It's just one word—alluding," Bucket said, nervously swallowing.

"Alluding...hmmm. I'm pretty sure we've never had that word.

Well, give us your sentence, and perhaps explain how the word fits in with the mystery theme."

Bucket read from her binder, "The suspect was alluding to her alibi when she said, 'You know I always go to bed by ten o'clock in the evening to watch the news.'" She looked at Mr. Harbicht hopefully.

"Nice work, you have made this word work with the mystery theme. Go ahead, you and Donald can be the ones to go on the word wall today." Donald and Bucket got up and carefully wrote their words in the appointed spaces. The bell rang for recess just as the class was putting away their books. Rowena and Providence hurried over to Bucket.

"Bucket, hurry up, we've got to go see who's on the list!" Rowena urged.

"I'm so excited," Providence said.

"OK, OK, I'm coming," Bucket responded, getting her jacket out of her locker and joining her friends.

There was a crowd of students huddled around the music bulletin board. Everyone seemed to be talking at once. Arthur was one of the students in the huddle. He turned to her and said, "Hey, sis, you did good!" and moved away so she could see what he was looking at.

And there it was: her name listed right next to the role of Mabel. She looked quickly to see what her friends had gotten. Rowena was cast as the Major General and Providence would be with her as a member of the girl's chorus. Everyone from the fifth and sixth grade classes was doing something. It was a small school with a small number of students in each grade, which meant everyone could be involved and that Mrs. Cauldwell could run her music rehearsals during class time.

Bucket and her two friends backed away from the crowd. Rowena and Providence started walking toward the big kids' exit, but Bucket said, "I'll catch up with you later...I just wanted to say something to Arthur".

Bucket walked down the little kids' hallway, thinking she had just missed him. But there was no Arthur in sight. So she used their exit anyway, making sure there were no playground supervisors by the door. There was usually one standing there, monitoring the students going in and out as they used the washroom. She quickly caught up with her friends.

"I don't know where he could be. I thought that I had just missed him. He should at least be outside," she said to Rowena and Providence.

"Well, he can't be far because nobody's allowed on the play apparatus. Mr. Bolen said," stated Rowena with authority.

"Aren't you excited about our parts in the musical?" Providence asked.

"I sure am!" Bucket said. "It will be really exciting to get the scripts after school. And then we have the whole week-end to look them over."

"You got a big part too!" Rowena exclaimed.

"I don't know about that. The major general is *huge*, Ro, and you get to sing that really cool song." Bucket gave her friend an impulsive hug. "And we get to be sisters, Pro," Bucket added, as she turned and gave Providence a hug.

"Gross, hugging in public!" they heard a voice say. It was Greg.

He was standing with his hands on his hips, glaring at them.

"Get lost, you little twerp," Rowena said. "Who needs your stupid comment? You're just jealous 'cause you don't have any friends."

"Wouldn't you like to know," Greg retorted.

"Just ignore him," Providence whispered, "and he'll go away". The girls turned their backs to the boy and started walking away. They didn't even look back. Greg lost interest and returned to the little kids' side of the tarmac.

Chapter Eight

Florence at Work

FLORENCE LOOKED AT HER WATCH FOR THE THIRD TIME, calculating when Miss Mitchell would be free to talk. After school on a Friday would be out of the question, so it had to be lunchtime. Florence had one more class to teach at the Fine Arts Centre, so she only had ten minutes to spare.

She ducked into her cubicle and dialed the number, pondering what she might say. She had met Miss Mitchell a few times during the year, usually at parent-teacher conferences, but they were not terribly in-depth. So far Arthur's year had been problem free, she had thought.

After speaking to the secretary and waiting a few precious minutes, Florence had Miss Mitchell on the line. "I really don't know how to say this, Miss Mitchell, but I'm a little worried about Arthur. Have you noticed any change in him lately?" Florence thought a general statement might be the easiest way into the subject.

"Oh, Mrs. Dunne, Arthur is one of my quietest students. I can't think off the top of my head that he's been any different lately. But I will definitely keep my eyes on him. I will make a note and let you know if there is anything at all," Miss Mitchell assured her.

"As I said, it could be absolutely nothing, but I wanted you to know my concerns. I would really appreciate it if you would let me know immediately if you see or hear anything. I didn't want to alarm you; I just wanted you to know, as a mother, what I was feeling." Florence hung up. She was certain that she had said far too much and not enough of anything.

Her boss, Elaine Savage caught up with her as she walked down the stairs to her next class.

"I hear congratulations are in order Flo," Elaine said, smiling.

"Thanks, Elaine. It was a real surprise to see my name on the list," Florence admitted.

"I hope you can get on at Moorland University. Then we wouldn't miss you next year," Elaine said.

"That would be fun, wouldn't it?" Florence agreed. "I'll be going into the fine details this week-end. Wish me luck!" Florence added as she turned to go into the drama room.

Elaine walked back to the staff room humming the theme from Beethoven's Fifth Symphony under her breath.

The Fine Arts Centre had been her brainchild. She had shepherded it along now for the past twenty years. Through government grants and sheer hard work, Elaine had grown the Centre from a venue for experimental fine-arts-in-education projects, to a vibrant year-long enterprise. Now teachers could bring their classes for a whole day of music, art and drama. They went back to their classrooms armed with follow-up plans and ideas as follow-up to the demonstration classes.. The Centre staff, just like Florence, were regular teachers, but each with a specialization in an area of fine arts.

Elaine had enjoyed assembling an eclectic staff. Some had years of experience teaching, while others brought the freshness and idealism of youth. One staff member had actually never been in the classroom, but was hired because she was mature and had such good references from her professors. It made for an oleo of sorts, but one that was never dull or pedestrian. Although...sometimes Elaine thought boring might be more restful.

Elaine's own area of expertise was music. She had been a choir director and run an extensive music program in many different schools. Travelling the globe was one of her passions and on one of these trips she had seen a centre for fine arts in England. In that centre there was a room each for dance, drama, art, and music. There was also a large central area with flexible seating for a gathering or a performance space. This inspired her, and on returning to Canada, Elaine discovered some government grants that would enable her to set up her own centre.

However, grant application was an art itself. Elaine had written so many that it was like second nature to her now. She'd had to renew the project every four years, and even in the interim years there were many-paged reports to prepare. After a while it was easier to anticipate the requirements by always having tabulations and observations on the go. The secretary manager of the centre was proficient at keeping monthly statistics, and each staff member had visiting teachers fill out a quick questionnaire. Some of these teachers even had their students write interesting thank-you notes back to the Centre. These notes were often poignant and sometimes a source of great hilarity.

Elaine chatted with the secretary, Carole Temple, who had just returned from her student supervision.

"What did you think about Florence's sabbatical?" Elaine asked.

"I'm really happy for her," Carole said, "but I'll miss her around the Centre. It's great news though," she added.

"She might be able to get on at the University of Moorland. I'm sure Florence wants to stick around because of the kids," offered Elaine.

"They're still young, but at least not too young. It will be a fun year for them all," Carole said. "Speaking of fun, I got some letters today from three classes that were here last week. Do you want to have a look, Elaine?" Carole took some papers out of a folder and passed them to her. Elaine sat down on one of the couches in their staff room and started to read them. After a while she looked up at Carole, who was working at her desk and asked,

"Do you have a moment?"

"Sure," Carole said quickly. Elaine was her boss, and rarely made unfair demands on her time.

"You have to hear some of these," Elaine said with a grin.

> *Thank you for teaching us art, music and dram. They are very good to learn. I hope to see you teachers again. You are very nice and you all have very nice smil. I hope you all had a nice day and I bet you always will.*

"That was cute, especially teaching dram and the smil. But the sentiment was quite sweet."

"Here's another," said Elaine.

> *I like the story about the cats and about your little brother it was funny. I could stay there forever.*

"Now that is really sweet," Carole commented.

"Shall I read you a couple more?" asked Elaine.

"Sure. I always like to hear what kids are thinking. Who knows what they walk away with after a day at the Fine Arts Centre?"

"OK. Let me see...here's one," Elaine said.

I liked the Music because it was wonderful.

"Now there's an endorsement!" Carole chuckled.

I liked the art because it was fun splashing the paint on the piece of paper. My favourite subject in school is art so I'm glad I wasn't sick that day. I hope it wasn't hard teaching us. Well thank you.

When we put the pant on our cat I was so excited. I was very hungry and I was glad We could eat lunch after.

Carole laughed. "Everyone has priorities! I remember when Jan Clayton used to work here. She had some pretty funny ones about painting. Have you got any more good ones?"

"Yes, of course. They are such a joy to read, aren't they?" Elaine said, continuing to dip into the pile of papers.

I like working in school very much, but I like to get away from it sometimes, and yesterday we didn't do any work so it was a fun day for me. I really do thank you.

The best thing we liked was when we got to make our own stories. The funniest part was when we got to act like squids. We hope we could come again.

"Wait a minute," said Elaine, with a big smile on her face, "this last one is the best yet!"

> *Dear Mrs. Temple. I like you very much. I liked you when you were in the lunch room. I like your hair Mrs. Temple. You are nice. I love you. With love to Mrs. Temple.*

"How's that for a fan letter, Carole?" laughed Elaine.

"It certainly is. I think I'll have it framed after we put a copy in the archives." Carole, eyes twinkling, turned back to the final administrative duties for the week's end. Elaine put all the letters back in the brown envelope.

"I'll be getting back to central office now. Have a great weekend." Elaine said, giving a brief wave.

"You, too. Take care." Carole returned to the final administrative duties for the week's end.

As Elaine walked down the hall she took a last look around. It gave her a great deal of satisfaction to know that the Fine Arts Centre was still a bee-hive of activity. She needed the formal feed-back from each school that took advantage of what the Centre had to offer, but she revelled in the informal thank-you letters from the children. That's when she and her staff knew that it was all worthwhile.

This year was the end of another grant cycle, and Elaine had no idea if any money would be forthcoming for the next four years. With government changes and the economy, it was hope against hope that kept her chugging along. She enjoyed the success of the Centre and was proud of all that they had done in the past twenty years. But she knew it was just a matter of time before the "experiment" would be mothballed.

Chapter Nine

It's Friday!

AFTER SCHOOL, FLORENCE WAS READY AND WAITING in the Toyota hatchback. Usually she was late, so she half expected Arthur and Bucket to be dawdling somewhere. But it was Friday, so maybe they were shooed out in good time. The crowds of parents and kids had dwindled, and finally Florence saw them in her rear view mirror. Since her talk with Miss Mitchell, she was wondering how the afternoon had been for Arthur and if Miss Mitchell was really going to watch what was going on. It was Friday after all—what did Florence expect?

As the two of them got into the car everything seemed fine, and Bucket was brimming over with enthusiasm.

"Mom, I got a part in the musical!" Bucket exclaimed.

"Wow, how good is that? What is the part, Bucket?"

"I'm playing Mabel. She's one of the major general's daughters. He has a lot of daughters! Mrs. Cauldwell has being telling all of us about it in music class," Bucket chattered rather breathlessly. "And I just got the script, see?" said Bucket pulled out a rather impressive sheaf of papers.

"That's going to be fun to read! I bet Arthur could help you learn your lines," Florence made sure they were belted in and then eased out into the traffic.

"We gotta go home to get Presto, don't forget," Arthur reminded. "We get to take her out to the Clayton's right?"

"That's right," Florence said. "Remember the last time? Presto got so excited when she saw the deer, we had a terrible time trying to call her back."

"She's a fast runner, Mom," Arthur said proudly.

They arrived at their home, a raised bungalow perched on a treed corner lot about fifteen blocks from the school. All three got out of the car quickly, grabbing backpacks, briefcases, and gym bags. As it was the end of the week, everything got piled up in the front entry awaiting organization the following day. Usually nothing had to be done with school or work on a Friday night. Except today, Bucket retrieved her script, not wanting it to get crinkled or torn.

Presto greeted each one of them with jumps and licks. Then she ran to the back door with Arthur right behind her to open it. Arthur picked up her leash when his mother said, "Don't forget that rag under the sink. She may get some mud on her paws. Actually, fill a bucket with water to wash those paws. We don't want Jan and Dorothy to get their house dirty, like ours is!"

"Oh, Mom," Arthur said, "they have a dog too!"

"I know they do, but they are the neatest, cleanest people I know. Whiskey may be a dog, but he's the cleanest dog In all of Moorland. Let's just say Presto's a bad influence, hmmm?" she added.

"OK. Here come's Presto already. Do you think she knows we're taking her out?" Arthur asked.

"She is a very sensitive dog," his mother said. "She may know that something's up. She always knows when you and Bucket are sick and spends the day with you on your bed."

"She is a really good dog, isn't she, Mom?" Arthur said, opening the door for Presto.

"She certainly is," agreed his mother. Florence and Arthur captured the dog at the back doorway and proceeded to put each paw in the pail of water and thoroughly dry it. Once released, Presto shook herself vigorously, whipping her tail in Arthur's face.

"Hey, Presto!" yelled Arthur. "Quit that, will you!" Florence got the dog blanket and put it by the leash. When they were driving anywhere with the dog, Presto always sat between Bucket and Arthur on the blanket while wearing the leash. Sometimes she would sit, but most of the time she stood with each of the kids holding onto her. She didn't bark but somehow couldn't relax enough to lie down and enjoy the ride. They rarely took her on a long trip, reasoning that it would be too stressful. She was much happier being dog-sat and had never been in a kennel.

They brought a bag of dog biscuits for Whiskey and Presto. Bucket had made some from scratch. She had done research for her science fair project in the winter and had made many batches, testing out different recipes on the dog. Her mother had frozen a few dozen. These were some of the last of the dog biscuits. Bucket had called this particular one "Liver Love." When she was making it, she had thought it smelled horrific, but Presto had relished the treats.

Once they were all back in the car, Florence made sure that Presto was secure on her dog blanket and that Bucket and Arthur were holding her firmly between them.

"We shouldn't be too late," their mother said. "I just have to make a quick stop to get a bottle of wine to go with dinner."

While Florence was in the Liquor Board Store, Bucket turned to Arthur.

"Where were you at recess Arthur? I just finished looking at the list for the musical and you simply disappeared. I couldn't find you outside either." Bucket hadn't wanted to ask him in front of their mother, for reasons she had yet to figure out.

"Really? You couldn't find me? Then it's working," Arthur said.

"What do you mean...it's working'?" Bucket asked.

"Me and Add. We have a disappearing routine we're working on. When we—" Arthur started to say, but stopped.

"There, that didn't take too long, did it?" Their mother got in the car, putting the bag of wine in the passenger's seat. Florence had never had Bucket or Arthur in the front seat of the car. She thought that it was much safer for both children in the back. Sometimes she felt like a chauffeur, but her sense of security outweighed any other misgivings she might have. The question of a dog being in the back-seat bothered her somewhat, but they so rarely took her far afield that Florence could rationalize not putting in a dog barrier.

Arthur turned to Bucket and put his finger to his lips. She raised her eyebrows, questioning. He shook his head. She nodded then, in acquiescence.

Chapter Ten

Presto and Whiskey's Great Adventure

THE WINDING ROAD THAT TOOK THEM to the Clayton's acreage was called Fox Valley Road. Florence had seen a few of those beautiful animals in their vicinity, but the "Valley" part of the name eluded her. The Clayton's house was one of about twenty along the road and was on the crest of a great foothill. Each piece of land came with a striking vista of the mountains beyond. The views were absolutely breathtaking on the long drive up to Jan and Dorothy's house. To the east was the Moorland skyline with its ever taller buildings and to the west were the Rockies.

Jan and Dorothy Clayton, two sisters who were both retired, had lived on their acreage for just a few years. In this short time they had planted aspens that lined the long drive, a grove of amur maple trees beside the house, pines to the north by their garage, and a row of lilacs right by the front deck. Florence noticed that the lilacs were starting to bud as they came up the set of stairs leading to the front door.

The door was already open. Whiskey raced ahead, bounding down to greet Presto, who was tugging at the leash. Bucket quickly unhooked the restraint so the dogs could be free to get to know one another again. Visits with the sisters were not infrequent, but a visit that included everyone in the family was a rare and special occasion.

The dogs remained outside, racing around, with the adults keeping a vigilant eye on their comings and goings. Foxes and coyotes were prevalent in the area, and the sisters had warned Florence and her children that coyotes especially worked as a team. One would lure the dog away, and then the rest of the pack would close around from behind. No one wanted that to happen. Bucket wondered if they should just keep the dogs inside until an adult could be with them, but the meal was ready and everyone was eager to hear the latest news.

They all sat down to dinner in what was part of a huge room adjacent to the kitchen. The table was set with white dishes with a red-and-green trim. Candles softly glowed from the centre piece. Florence had set her opened bottle of wine on the table. Bucket and Arthur sat beside each other, opposite their mother. Jan and Dorothy took either end of the table, with Jan being closest to the kitchen. She had an amazing collection of cook books and was always trying something new and different.

"Wherever did you get the pussy willows?" Florence asked, gesturing to the centre piece.

"We discovered them on our walk this morning with Whiskey," explained Dorothy. "We were happy to see them. It was such a cold winter, wasn't it?"

"Yup," Arthur said. "It was so cold that the Arrow River is still frozen."

"And some of our backyard, underneath the big spruce, is still frozen as well. I expect last night's rain will have helped the thaw," Florence offered.

"Mom has some good news too!" Bucket announced.

"Maybe we should serve the food first. We don't want it to get cold," Florence said, not willing to have all the attention land on her just yet. "What is that delicious smell, Jan?" Florence asked.

"It's called bobotie. It's really a crazy recipe. I thought you might be in the mood for a bit of culinary adventure. I won't tell you what's in it yet," she teased.

"I know," Arthur said, "we have to guess!"

"That's right," Dorothy agreed. "But I will tell you that this time, Jan assures me, there are no monkey brains in the recipe!"

"Ugh, Dorothy," Bucket groaned. "Now I can't eat it!"

But they all dug in, and there were many gratifying sounds and words of praise for the cook and her unusual recipe. Every now and then Arthur glanced out the window, keeping track of Presto and Whiskey. By the time the dishes were being cleared up for dessert, Arthur noticed that the dogs had finally played themselves out and were sitting on the top deck looking out toward the river.

"Well mom," Bucket said, "are you going to tell them or not?"

As they sat down in front of their dishes of ice cream sundaes, Florence said, "I've been given a sabbatical for next year!" She looked at Jan and Dorothy to see what they would say.

"That's so exciting, Flo! You must be over the moon," responded Jan. "And are you kids both happy for your mom?" she asked, looking from Bucket to Arthur.

"I'm really proud of mom for getting it," Bucket said with a big smile.

"It's cool," Arthur said, "but I don't know why everybody's so excited. She'll have to go back to school for a whole year!" He looked at them all to see if anyone understood his puzzlement on the subject.

"You see, Arthur," said Dorothy, "sometimes school can be a break for a hard-working adult. It's a chance to recharge the batteries, see different faces, and explore new ideas."

"And she might have enough time in her schedule to go to your school and be a parent helper. I'd bet you'd like that!" proposed Jan.

"I guess so. But she'd still have to go to school and write exams and stuff," Arthur said, remaining unconvinced.

Everyone just laughed. They knew that there was nothing they could say to convince Arthur. He had never been as enamoured of school as his sister, Bucket. It's not that the work had ever been difficult for him. Perhaps the opposite was the real reason—he had never been fully or creatively challenged at school.

"Does it mean you'll be studying at a different university? We only have Moorland U. here, Florence," said Dorothy. It was a casual comment, but Florence held her breath. She had yet to open up that possibility with her children.

"Funny you should mention that. I'm going to try to get my application in on Monday. I just picked up the forms today on the way to the children's school. I never studied at Moorland U., so it will be a different experience—that's for sure."

"It will be a great year for all of you, I'm sure," Jan said with her customary positive attitude.

"And...are you ready for it?" Florence intoned. "We have spectacular news of a Bucket variety. Tell them, Bucket."

"I got a part in the school musical," Bucket said. "My name will be Mabel and my best friend Rowena is going to be the major general!"

"Now that sounds like a Gilbert and Sullivan musical," Dorothy said. "Which one is it?" she asked her sister Jan.

"Oh, that's one of my favourites. It's called *The Pirates of Penzance.* There are lots of pirates, and of course the major general and one of his daughters Mabel. I believe there are lots of policemen as well." Although Jan was a retired art teacher, she had once taught in England and had had the chance to see many theatre and musical productions while she worked there.

Arthur had gotten up during the last part of Jan's comments. He was looking out the window, searchingly. He turned around to them now and said with a little concern,

"I can't see Whiskey or Presto." The two dogs were always on the go. This was nothing unusual, but Arthur was a bit worried because of all the talk of coyotes being in the area.

"We're finished dinner anyway Arthur," confirmed Dorothy. "Why don't you and Bucket go outside and check everything out. I think you will remember their favourite spots."

With that Bucket and Arthur grabbed their jackets and went out the big front door. They looked, but the dogs were not to be found on any part of the main deck. Bucket started calling.

"Prestoooooooo! Whiskeeeeeeeeeey!" she yelled, almost singing their names.

Arthur ran down the front steps and across the huge yard. The sisters had a sit-down mower that they used to cut the grass of the two acres immediately next to their home. Just last year they had decided to let the rest of the acreage go to natural grasses, with a mowed pathway down to a rudimentary one-room shelter they called the fox house. The hut was perched on the edge of their property. The land fell steeply off to the south and west of it, so the fox house got the brunt of every wind that whisked or roared through the property.

"Let's go to the fox house and look for them there!" Arthur yelled, already propelling himself down the mowed walkway.

Bucket was on her way, running pell-mell down the sloped yard to the pathway beyond. She continued to yell the dogs' names as she ran, catching up to Arthur just as he got to the look-out.

And there they saw them. Both dogs had their noses under the east side of the shelter. The fox house didn't have any foundation, just concrete footings. Presto and Whiskey were growling and sniffing, running from one corner of the hut to the other.

"Boy, I'm sure glad we found them," Arthur laughed with relief.

"Yeah, I was kinda worried too," breathed Bucket, still huffing and puffing from her run.

"I wonder what they're trying to get?"

"It could be mice. Remember the last time they disappeared? We found them trying to get into the wood pile beside the garage. They were barking something terrible!"

"Or maybe it is a fox! Isn't that how this got its name?" he asked, gesturing to the hut.

"That's right," Bucket confirmed. "Dot and Jan came down one day to have lunch inside the shelter. And when they stepped out the door to go back home, a fox was standing just a few feet away from them, snarling."

"Boy, that must have been something! I wish I coulda been there," Arthur said a little wistfully.

"You're crazy, you know that, Arthur? Of course they were

scared. They could have been bitten and then maybe gotten rabies." Bucket was indignant. People just didn't seem to know the perils of wildlife. Now she was anxiously looking at Presto and Whiskey sniff around the base of the shelter.

"Didn't they see the baby foxes?"

"Yes they did. After a while—they watched with binoculars from the top of the lawn and behind the tall grasses so they couldn't be seen." Bucket gestured to their vantage point.

"I can't remember what happened to them," Arthur said.

"They put moth balls underneath all of the walls and then the next day they were gone." As Bucket said this, she felt a little wistful too. She loved animals in the wild and thought it would have been amazing to have seen a whole family of foxes.

"C'mon, Presto! Come on girl! Let's go home!" Arthur said, trying to coax Presto to stop sniffing and running around. Bucket tried the same with Whiskey. The Clayton's dog may have been small, but right now it was determined and stubborn. No amount of cajoling for either dog seemed to have any effect.

"I'll go get some dog biscuits," Arthur said.

"Dummy me!" Bucket exclaimed. "I still have my Liver Loves in my pocket!" She brought out the bag filled with a dozen dark-coloured dog biscuits. Bucket had even cut them into bone shapes. She took out a few for Arthur and herself and put the reserve back in her pocket.

Both Bucket and Arthur were experienced in trying to entice a dog using a treat. The trick was *not* to give the treat immediately. If that happened, the dog would just go back to whatever their bad behaviour was at the moment. It had to be like the proverbial carrot on a stick—just enough to get their interest, but not enough to satisfy them.

Bucket tried to get Whiskey's attention. She had to bend down and put the biscuit right in front of the dog. That worked! Whiskey actually turned away from the fox house. Now Bucket had to judge the critical distance at which she could back up toward the house with the biscuit in hand, while still having the dog's attention. Arthur watched with amusement as Bucket slowly backed up the slope to the house.

By now Presto noticed that her partner in crime was no longer with her. It wasn't that difficult for Arthur to encourage Presto to follow him. Presto had already sampled Bucket's treats when she was doing her experiments, so she didn't need much persuasion to follow something so enticingly familiar.

In no time at all the two dogs were back on the lawn next to the house. Now Bucket and Arthur gave the dogs their well-deserved treats. Whiskey knew how to beg, so Bucket gave him another treat. Presto got a second one as well, even though she had never been taught such behaviours as "sit" and "heel."

Chapter Eleven

The Calm Before

THE ADULTS EMERGED FROM THE HOUSE just as the sun started to set. Bucket and Arthur had the two dogs seated quietly on the top deck of the house. Both dogs were quite subdued from their exertions.

"Where did you find the dogs?" asked Florence.

"They were at the fox house," said Arthur.

"Now I wonder what they were up to there?" Jan murmured, as she walked over and knelt down to pat Whiskey.

"We don't really know," Bucket explained. "They were sure excited about something."

"Yeah, they were barking and running around and sniffing," Arthur added.

"You were lucky to get them to pay attention to you at all," commented Dorothy. "It's a wonder they came back to the house with you."

"Well, you know, it's magic," Arthur said mysteriously.

"No it's not. It's my new recipe for dog biscuits," corrected Bucket.

"Hey, why'd ya have to spoil it, sis?" Arthur teased. "Just don't tell them the name. They might not give it to Whiskey if you do."

Bucket stood up and took the bag of biscuits out of her pocket.

"Here you are," she said, handing the bag to Jan. "They're called Liver Love. I was going to give them to you anyway, but some of them got eaten before I got the chance!"

"Arthur may be right," Jan said with a grimace. "It's a good thing the dogs are the only ones eating these!"

"You know mom's a liver lover," Arthur said, enjoying the alliteration and exaggerating it.

"It's true," Florence admitted. "My father induced me to eat liver when I was a kid. Sometimes we even had liver casserole." Everyone groaned, except Florence.

"Well, gang," she said, "I hate to break up the party, but I think it's time to hit the road."

"It was wonderful to see you again," Dorothy said.

"It's been far too long since we've all been together," added Jan.

"Thanks so much for the wonderful evening," Bucket said.

"When you want to do more adventure cooking, we'll be up for it," Arthur said, adding, "Just no liver OK?" They all laughed.

"Have fun at your rehearsals, Bucket," Jan said.

"Thanks," Bucket said shyly.

With that, Bucket and Arthur hugged the Clayton sisters and got into the car with Presto. Florence hung back momentarily and said to Jan and Dorothy, "Please don't worry too much about what I've told you about Arthur. I'm sure it's nothing. And thanks, Jan, for considering helping with the backdrop for the musical. I know they can really do with artistic guidance at that school!" She hugged both sisters and moved to the car.

Jan called out, "Good luck with your application. You can use me as a reference if you want."

"You are just too good to me. Thanks again for the lovely meal—it made Friday bearable!" Florence, smiling and waving, got into the car. Jan and Dorothy stood on their top deck, waving until the car turned onto Fox Valley Road.

Dorothy bent down to Whiskey and said, "I think you're ready for a good night's rest, aren't you?" Jan opened the front door, and both sisters and the dog went inside.

As Florence drove down Fox Valley Road, the sun had set deep behind the mountains and the peaks had turned an indigo blue. The sky was now a muted, blush rose. There were no cars about, and the gravel road hadn't quite dried from yesterday's rain. Their dog was actually sitting now between the two children.

"Mom, I think Presto may have gotten some burrs at the Clayton's," said Bucket, petting Presto and exploring the long dog hair on her back and sides.

"You and Arthur know what to do. Gently ease them out of her fur and put them in this Kleenex," said their mother, passing back a few tissues to Arthur and Bucket. "By the time we get home, you might have quite a few out. We'll get the rest when we're home."

"Mom, is Jan really gonna help with the musical?" Arthur asked.

"Well, she said she'd work on the backdrops that your class will be doing. Miss Mitchell put that announcement in the last school newsletter. It will be a really big undertaking! Actually, Jan doesn't usually go into schools anymore. This is a first! She's going to call Miss Mitchell on Monday. We'll see what happens."

"It would be cool if she came to the school," Bucket said.

"Yeah, it would be...but she's only gonna come to *my* class," Arthur said in his best teasing manner.

"Oh yeah, you just think you're so smart, don't you!?" challenged Bucket, poking Arthur.

"Am too! What of it?" he said, poking her back. At this point Presto gave a little bark, protesting being in the middle of their carrying on.

As the car travelled toward Moorland, Florence started thinking about all the decisions that were just around the corner. She could hear Bucket and Arthur in the back seat, but she never worried about their behaviour. When Arthur was born, Bucket had taken to him immediately. Florence had a photograph of her two-year-old little girl bending over the newborn, encircling him with her arms and giving him a gentle kiss. It was one of those moments, so pure and spontaneous, that had somehow characterized their relationship ever since.

As they drove along, Florence thought about the sabbatical, her job, the children's schooling, and the joint custody she shared with her ex-husband. Then her focus shifted just to her son. Because Arthur was three when she split up with Jean, he hadn't had a male role model for a while. There was no-one from her immediate family in the city. Florence's father lived on the West Coast with her step-mother. Her sister's husband was too far away. And Wilt was not interested in her children's lives the way her sister was. She did have some good friends in Moorland who had attentive husbands, so they at least were in his life.

Florence was starting to realize that Arthur was surrounded by female role models. He had also been taught since he was a toddler to respect Bucket and to resolve differences with talking rather than hitting. She was happy that her two children got along so famously, but she hadn't wanted Arthur to be a complete pacifist. She worried that he had missed out on some crucial teaching concerning the maleness of the world—and of the playground. He had never been shown that it was sometimes OK to "stick up your dukes" and fight for yourself. Florence continually struggled with making a complete and safe home for her children. She never wanted them to lose out, but she could not be both mother and father.

Florence gave her head a shake. This wasn't a productive line of thinking at all. Parenting perfection was not in the cards for anyone! And besides, she felt lucky to have so many good things in her life. She had a great job that was never the same from day to day. She enjoyed the staff she worked with, and her boss was definitely exceptional—talented and completely committed to arts education.

Florence knew that the friends she had in Moorland kept her going too. Her sister's support had been tremendous, even though she lived in a different province. But most of all she felt blessed by her two children. She had Bucket and Arthur in her life. Even after a demanding day, coming home to be with them was always a balm for the soul. She enjoyed each stage they were going through and anticipated what they would say or do next. She had heard about single parents becoming "friends" with their children and taking on behaviours that were a bit child-like themselves. Florence hoped that would not be her fate, especially when her kids became teenagers. Florence couldn't conceive of being the kind of mom to dress up the same as her daughter. That thought alone kept her smiling until she drove up to the house.

Chapter Twelve

Gabriel and Gwyneth—Part 2

As soon as they got home, all three turned their attention to Presto. They had her stand still while they carefully worked on her fine hair, removing the little twigs and burrs. Her feathered feet picked up bits and pieces too, although she had been trying to clean these herself during the drive back to the city. Bucket gave the dog a thorough brushing, which was normally done outside. However, Presto really needed the grooming, so it couldn't wait until morning. Arthur caught the black hairs and put them in a bag with everything else they had collected.

That night Bucket and Arthur, along with Presto between them, were found patiently waiting on their mother's bed. They were in their pajamas ready to hear the next instalment of the story. Florence had been in the kitchen, putting away dishes. She was surprised to see them there, thinking that it had been a long day for each of them and that they would be snuggled down in their own rooms.

"What's this about?" she asked the duo.

"C'mon mom," Arthur said. "You never finished it."

"Finished what?" asked their mother innocently.

"The story of Gwyneth and Gabriel. You've got to finish it

tonight or we're not going to bed!" Bucket said determinedly.

"Yup, that's right. No sleep *all* night long," Arthur challenged.

"Alright! I just thought you were both too old for these stories," their mother teased.

"I don't know if we'll ever be too old for the G and G stories, mom," said Bucket, patting a place between her and Arthur. So their mother sat down, composed herself, and resumed the story.

"*Gwyneth was eyeing the wriggling sack with some trepidation. She knelt down beside Gabriel to get a better look. By the time their mother got to the spot, Gabriel was already starting to open the sack, but he was having trouble. It was covered in snow, and the knots had become stiff with the cold. Their mother trained the flashlight on the bundle so they could see what they were doing, although the snow was falling so thickly that it was still difficult.*

"*'I think whatever it is must still be alive!' exclaimed Gwyneth.*

"*'I know, I'll take off my mitts,' Gabriel said, ripping them off and throwing them on the ground. At last the knots loosened. The strange sounds that they had heard got suddenly loud and pitiful.*

"*'Careful. We still don't know what's in there!' cautioned their mother.*

"*'Oh Mom, look!' Gwyneth cried.*

"*'A whole pile of baby kittens!' Gabriel said and took one up in his arms.*

"*'Oh my goodness, children!' their mother said anxiously. 'We've got to get these little ones in a warm place! How many are there?'*

"*'I think there are nine,' Gwyneth said, who had the sack open on the ground.*

"*'They are very tiny. I think we could each take three inside our jackets,' their mother instructed. 'And leave that wretched sack where it is!'*

"So, Gabriel picked up two more kittens while his sister and mother picked up the remainder, being careful to fit them ever so gently inside their jackets. Gwyneth took her arms out of her sleeves so she could hold onto them directly.

"No-one could hang onto the flashlight, but there was enough illumination from the stark whiteness of the fallen snow that they could make their way home. Their pathway through the woods was already getting obscured. Any later and they may have had difficulty. Their mother took the lead with Gwyneth, and Gabriel brought up the rear. It was a slow and somewhat noisy procession. The kittens were mewing, but Gwyneth had one lively kitten that was already digging its paws into her sweater. She reacted to this with little exclamations of 'ouch!' as they trudged back to their home.

"When they finally got onto the back porch, they took turns taking off their boots and bringing the kittens into the kitchen. Their mother quickly got a box and lined it with an old flannelette sheet that she used to wrap around throats when anyone had a bad cough. There was enough of the sheet to make a double layer so that it would be extra warm.

"The mewing was reaching a crescendo. Three of the kittens seemed a little weak, but the others were definitely making their needs known. After heating up some milk on the stove, Gwyneth and Gabriel took turns feeding them with an eye dropper. The smallest one had a floppy ear and really needed encouragement to eat. Gabriel said,

"'Hey, that's the first one I picked up. I carried him here. He really is little.'

"'Then you have to take extra care with that one. Sometimes the runt of the litter gets pushed aside by its brothers and sisters,' explained their mother.

"'That's cruel,' Gwyneth objected.

"'Sorry. I didn't make the rules. That's just how things happen in nature, but we've got the kittens now, Gwyneth,' she comforted.

"'Why were they all in that sack, mom?' Gabriel asked.

"'I think farmers do that, don't they?' Gwyneth said.

"'Yes, sometimes. If they don't want those mouths to feed, that's what happens. They probably thought the woods would do just as well as drowning them in a pond, and that's how we came to find them,' said their mother.

"That night, Gwyneth and Gabriel fed the kittens twice more. A heating lamp was found and positioned above the box. Luckily Gwyneth and Gabriel's mom worked from their home, so she could feed the kittens every hour the next day while they were in school.

"One month of alternating joy and mayhem went by. Gwyneth and Gabriel worked hard to play with each kitten so that they all got their share of hugs and play time. Playtime was where the mayhem came in. Even though they were still comparatively small, each kitten had found a way to circumvent their cardboard enclosure. After two weeks they were in three different boxes so it wasn't too crowded. Mealtime got a lot easier too, but taking them to the veterinarian was hysterical. It was also very expensive to get shots for nine kittens.

"Finally the day came when the prospect of adopting out each lovely fur ball had to be contemplated.

"'Gabriel and Gwyneth,' their mother began, 'I know how much you like these kittens, but we really can't afford to keep them.'

"'I have a plan, mom,' Gwyneth volunteered. 'I'm going to write an article for our school newspaper about how we found the kittens in the bag. I'll advertise that they're up for adoption too.'

"'And I'm going to photograph them with your camera, Mom. I was

thinking that I'd do a group shot, and then a separate one for each of the kittens,' Gabriel said proudly.

"'*Hmmm. It sounds to me like you two had this all organized before I even thought of saying anything!' their mother chuckled.*

"'*We would also like to ask you if we could keep one,' Gwyneth said.*

"'*Now that's a more difficult decision. You would both have to promise to take care of the kitten,' their mother said sternly.*

"'*Sure we would mom,' said Gabriel with enthusiasm. 'Me-n Gwyn would do it together.'*

"'*And who would be in charge of the kitty litter,' their mother inquired pointedly.*

"'*We'd both be. Honest. We would take turns doing the litter and feeding the cat. We promise. Right, Gabe?' Gwyneth asked, looking to her brother for reassurance.*

"'*Yes. We already talked about it, mom, and we agreed,' Gabriel said firmly.*

"'*I can certainly tell that you've already talked about it! Give me some time to think about the costs and everything,' their Mother added. 'Which kitten did you have in mind?'*

"'*We both thought the one with the floppy ear. He's the runt of the litter and he needs the most care right now,' Gwyneth explained.*

"'*We've got a name too!' Gabriel said. 'He's going to be called Van Gogh'*

◇ ◇ ◇

"I know! I know why!" Bucket exclaimed, interrupting the story.

"Know why what?" her mother innocently asked.

"Why they gave the kitten that name," said Bucket patiently.

"Aw, everybody knows. Van Gogh cut off his ear, didn't he,"

Arthur said impatiently, wanting his mother to continue the story.

"Yes, that's right Arthur. Now may I continue?" their mother asked. They both nodded their heads vigorously in agreement.

◇ ◇ ◇

"So it happened that Gwyneth wrote the story about the abandoned kittens. Gabriel had lots of fun taking the photographs. Some of the pictures simply had to be action shots. The kittens were all calicoes, which made the group photo showy but out of focus because a fur-ball had moved. Van Gogh was excluded in the pictures. The children were hoping their mother would decide to keep him for themselves. Finally the article appeared in the school newspaper, complete with Gabriel's pictures.

"The reaction was astounding. There was a general outrage at the whole cat-in-the-bag phenomenon. One of the parents from Gabriel and Gwyneth's school was a reporter for the city-wide newspaper. He decided to do an article himself on the kittens and even used some of Gabriel's photographs, in addition to interviewing the family. They had no trouble finding homes for each of the kittens because of all the publicity.

"But best of all, people started to send Gabriel and Gwyneth money to off-set all of the veterinarian bills they'd had to pay. With their mother's permission the children decided, instead, to set up a fund in Van Gogh's name. All the money raised would go to their local SPCA. This last action of theirs prompted yet another article, which brought more money for the fund.

"And Van Gogh was a very happy cat in the Gabriel and Gwyneth household."

"That was a really good story," Bucket said appreciatively.

"Yeah, I liked that one too. When can we get a cat?" Arthur asked.

"I think Presto is enough of a pet for this family," their mother said, petting the dog affectionately. Bucket and Arthur trundled off to bed. Florence put Presto out one last time.

After everyone was settled for the night, Florence got into her bed and took up her latest murder mystery. Her sister had gotten her interested in reading this genre when Florence was first on her own. Because she had trouble getting to sleep during the nights following the turmoil of the separation from her husband, Edie had suggested that she try reading mysteries. It was cheaper than taking sleeping pills and far more interesting. It had proved to be the one thing that put Florence to sleep. After just a few pages, her eyes would grow heavy, and then she would turn out the light. Sleep followed effortlessly.

Some of her friends had suggested that she had a ghoulish mind or was becoming demented in her single-hood, but Florence thought that each mystery took her on a journey of discovery. There was usually an identifiable protagonist: the detective, police agent, lawyer, or some other such seeker of the truth who was also morally principled. The antagonists varied, but they all came with a set of characteristics that included one or more flaws of corruption. The struggle between the opposing forces was satisfying. Florence's own struggles faded into the background while reading of such visceral contests of will and wit.

The rest of the week-end went by quickly. On Saturday night Bucket and Arthur stayed with their dad; his wife, Marie, and their baby daughter, Geneviève. Florence did all the household chores, even hanging the sheets out on the line in the backyard. She took Presto for a long walk in the meandering park near their home. The spring wind was refreshing and the pathways were not too wet.

Florence spent Sunday working on her application for graduate studies at the University of Moorland. She also wrote a letter to Anna Sexton's University asking for application forms, just in case. The sabbatical had stated that the year was to be devoted to full-time study but had not stated anything other than that. She knew some of her colleagues had taken three classes or their equivalent over the course of ten months, which was also considered a complete program for the purposes of a sabbatical. Florence knew that if her bid to start a master's degree did not pan out, she could also simply enrol in three interesting classes. It gave her a bit of leeway, and for that she was thankful. If an opportunity to study outside of Moorland arose, there would be a whole truckload of decisions to make.

Chapter Thirteen

Arthur Alone

MONDAY MORNING DAWNED BRIGHT AND BRISK. When Florence dropped the children off at the school, Bucket was excited about starting to rehearse the musical. Arthur seemed pleased as well. He had done a painting at his dad's that he wanted to show his teacher. Florence thought that it was a particularly good one of a space ship in the outer atmosphere with the Earth spinning beneath it. The space ship even looked metallic and shimmery, with some detailing Arthur had probably spent a great deal of time executuing. The background was in shades of indigo and deep, deep blue. Earth was a teal colour.

"Don't forget," his mother said, "stay at Bucket's rehearsal after school. I'll pick you up afterwards. And please remember to bring back that painting, Arthur."

"Yes mom," he said. "I won't forget it." And he turned and ran into the school. Florence hoped that all was well in Arthur's world.

That day the Centre's classes were particularly rambunctious. Sometimes after a week-end children were quite subdued, having worn themselves out playing. The three classes were all grade six students and it seemed like spring fever had hit most of them. However, they liked sharing their improvisations with each other.

Florence had to make sure that this sharing time brought out the best in each student, both as a participant and an observer. She was very much a coach in each class: encouraging, editing, and challenging each student to do their best. It was definitely not the kind of teaching that allowed an educator to give "seat work."

As Florence drove to the school to pick up Bucket and Arthur, she mulled over the lively classes she had taught, but also the conversation she'd had over the phone with one of her potential advisers in the education department at the University of Moorland. It seemed that with her background she would have a better chance at getting into the MA program than the M Ed. It would mean a new application that would have to be in by the end of the week. However, Florence thought that wouldn't be too difficult because her curriculum vitae was in order, as were her transcripts and letters of reference. There was a nice, thick file folder at home with the papers she would need. She had put it all together for her sabbatical application. If Jan Clayton was going to add another letter, she would be happy to include it.

As Florence turned the corner onto Bannister Drive she noticed that the school ground was deserted except for a lone figure who was sitting in the middle of the grassy sport's field. As she parked her car and got out, she realized it was Arthur. She thought for sure that she had told him to wait inside the school until Bucket was finished with her rehearsal.

"Arthur," she called out. But he didn't move or acknowledge her. Her mild annoyance turned to extreme concern. Florence walked quickly to where Arthur was sitting. She noticed that his back pack was on the ground and its contents lay in a jumble around him. She quietly picked up all the bits and pieces and placed them in the pack. Then she sat in front of Arthur and put her hands on his shoulders.

"What on earth happened, Arthur?" His mother strove to sound calm and relaxed.

"Sorry, Mom," he said in a quiet voice.

"What could you possibly be sorry about?" she asked, perplexed.

"I know you told me to stay at the rehearsal, but I thought it would be fun to play outside for a while," Arthur explained.

"You know I trust you to make good judgments. I'm sure it would have been OK. But that's not what this is about. What happened, Arthur?" his mother asked, as gently as she could without appearing anxious.

"I didn't see them coming. They grabbed my backpack and threw me around. They wouldn't let me get up," he said haltingly, almost in tears.

"You know what, Arthur? We're going to get up now and we're going home. Come on." And with that, Florence picked up his back pack and walked with him to the car, her arm around his shoulders. She did not want Arthur to see her very real concern. She didn't know why, but she didn't want him to dwell on whatever had happened. Her one desire was to get him home as quickly as possible and to bring him to safety.

"What about the painting?" his mother gently asked, as they neared her car.

"I gave it to Bucket after school," he said softly, as he slid into the back seat.

"All right. I'll be back with Bucket in a sec." Florence strode into the school. She was suddenly angry at Miss Mitchell and the staff of Bannister Elementary. How could they let such things happen, even if it *was* after school? She noticed the rehearsal was breaking up in the gym, so she motioned to Bucket, who picked up her things and joined her immediately.

"What's wrong, mom?" Bucket asked. "You look really upset."

"I just want to get home Bucket. Let me help you with Arthur's painting." Florence took the painting. They walked quickly out of the school before any of the other students in the musical rehearsal left. Florence knew that she couldn't trust herself to talk with anyone at the moment because she was just too emotional.

"Everything OK, bro?" Bucket asked Arthur, wondering what was going on.

"I'm OK sis. I'm always OK right?" Arthur said, with all the courage he could muster.

Bucket didn't know what to think. Something was up, but her mother's silence spoke volumes, and she knew it would be better to keep quiet. From past experience Bucket knew that their mother would tell them what was happening when she was ready. Bucket hoped that it wasn't about her mother's application to the University of Moorland.

As they sat at the dinner table early that evening, Florence said, "Arthur is being bullied at school. Did you know that, Bucket?" She said it rather roughly, as if Bucket should have known about it all along.

"Of course not, mom! I didn't know at all. Are you all right, Arthur?" she asked with concern.

"Sorta," Arthur said simply.

"I'm going to call Miss Mitchell tomorrow and let her know. Were they from your class, Arthur? Can you give me their names?" Even as Florence spoke, she realized she might not be asking the right questions.

"Mom, you can't do that. If Miss Mitchell knows and does something about it…it'll get worse," Arthur protested.

"Arthur, this isn't right," his mother said. "Those boys have to be accountable for their actions." Even as she said it, she could see that Arthur wasn't going to tell her the names of his tormentors.

"It's not just me," Arthur said in a small voice.

"What? Who else have they targeted?" she asked.

"It's always me and Add, and sometimes Lance," he said.

"Thank you, love. I will get to the bottom of this, Arthur. You have my word." Bucket and Arthur looked down at their plates. Their Mother was silent. And then they heard a whimper. It was a sad, sorrowful sound coming from under the table.

"It's Presto, Mom," Bucket said. "She knows we're unhappy."

And sure enough, Presto was curled up by Arthur's feet under the table. Arthur bent down, and the dog licked Arthur's hand enthusiastically.

"It's OK. Presto. I'm OK." Arthur said soothingly. Presto answered with a few sharp barks, where-upon everyone laughed. Florence served the dinner, and the conversation naturally went on to other matters.

Chapter Fourteen

Needed—One Avenging Angel

THAT NIGHT FLORENCE STOOD IN THE DOORWAY to Arthur's bedroom and looked at him as he lay sleeping next to Presto. She was absolutely determined that he not feel the victim. Going through her divorce had taught her that strength lay in feeling you were in control of some of the circumstances of a suddenly chaotic life. She didn't want Arthur ever to feel that he couldn't handle a difficult situation. Bucket had been lucky to have fairly good teachers in her schooling so far. Florence also felt that it was easier for a girl on the playground, although she suddenly remembered that in her own childhood kids would tease her about her last name: "Dunne, Dunne, you dirty bum." Florence's parents couldn't protect her from those jibes, and yet she had come out of her schooling career relatively unscathed.

She decided to call her sister. Edie was able to give her feedback when she needed it, although Edie also had her share of challenges. Her husband Wilt, was eccentric and a workaholic. Her in-laws were very demanding as well, although the flip side was that they were also attentive. Edie had always enjoyed being with her in-laws because their European background was so different from her own. Florence and the children had fun visiting with Edie's in-laws as well—and for the same reason. Meals there were always formal and gourmet. Edie was an excellent cook too and had taken to re-creating many of Wilt's family recipes.

Edie answered on the third ring and Florence quickly related the events of the day. She hadn't realized how upset she was about everything until it spilled out all in a rush. When she finally stopped, she was almost out of breath and tearing up.

"Wow, Flo, you've had a terrible day," Edie said. "I am really sorry to hear about Arthur. Can't you just take him out of the school?"

"I don't think that would be a good idea. I don't want Arthur to feel he can't manage this, unless of course, it's way bigger than just a few incidents of bullying. Honestly, it never crossed my mind, Edie."

"I'm so glad Wilt and I didn't have kids. I'd be worried about them all the time. I'd probably have been one of those mothers who keeps her child on a very short leash."

"It is a balance that's difficult to get right," Florence admitted. "One moment you want to protect them from any kind of obstacles they might meet in life, and the next moment you realize that they need to experience problems on their own in order to learn how to solve them. Do you think I protect them too much Edie?"

"Of course you do—especially since the divorce," Edie said. Her policy was to speak the truth. She didn't believe in sugar-coating something that should be taken seriously. Edie loved Bucket and Arthur and didn't want anything to happen to them. She understood Florence's fierce protectiveness even though she wasn't a mother herself.

"Um, that's good to hear," Florence said, completely crestfallen.

"Look, I know you'll work it out. If I were there I'd be the avenging angel and come down on those little buggers who did that to Arthur—so fast they wouldn't know which way was up!" Edie said angrily.

"Wow! I'm glad we've got you in our corner, Edie. That image will stay with me while I go undercover and try to figure out just who those little buggers are," Florence said, almost laughing.

"Darn right!" Edie exclaimed. "And while this angel's at it, I'd like to string up Arthur's teacher. She's obviously of the 'hear nothing—see nothing' variety," Edie snorted with disdain.

"Miss Mitchell seems like a nice person. I think she's just got her hands full with so many boys in her class," Florence countered.

"There you go again, Flo! You're making excuses for incompetence. She's paid to take care of everyone in her class," Edie said with vehemence.

"I know you're right. I just never thought about it that way. She's getting a call from me first thing tomorrow, although I don't have any names for her. At least I can tell her about the incident with Arthur after school today. There's something definite now, not just a niggling feeling I've had," Florence said.

"That's for sure!" Edie agreed. "Now what happened to your application for the University of Moorland? It went right out of my mind when you started talking about Arthur."

Florence told her sister about submitting an application to a different department at the same university. She didn't go into too much detail because she didn't know how the application process would be different. Edie was very encouraging, but pressed Florence to complete the paper-work in short order. Deadlines were looming, and she didn't want her sister to lose out.

"Before you go, Edie, are you and Wilt still going to come at Easter?"

There was a pause at the other end, and then Edie said, "I'm still working on it. I know, I know...I thought it was definite, but you know how business can be. I'll keep you posted. Take care and good luck!"

"Thanks for listening. Love you," Florence said.

"Love you too, you goof!"

Florence slowly replaced the receiver, deep in thought. She was turning over the possibility of informing Jean of Arthur being bullied. Although they were divorced and Jean had another family, they usually attended parent-teacher interviews together. Florence made sure that he had a copy of Bucket's and Arthur's report cards. It was important to her that the children's father was aware of their progress in school. When it was his week-end to see them, she tried to encourage him to help out with their assignments. But now his infant daughter took up a great deal of his time, in addition to his fledgling carpentry business. Perhaps she'd see how far she'd get with phone calls and her own investigation before she involved him on the issue.

Just as Florence was closing up the house for the night and giving Presto one last visit to the backyard, the phone rang.

"Sorry to bother you so late, Florence," Jan Clayton said, "but I was busy in the studio and time just slipped away."

"Not to worry Jan, I wasn't under the covers just yet."

"I talked to that teacher at the children's school today. I'll be there tomorrow and then once or twice a week after that. It should be fun. They might even give me an honorarium," Jan said.

"That's great, Jan. I can hardly wait to tell them tomorrow morning. They certainly should give you something for doing such yeoman work," Florence stated. "By the end of it, you may want a medal!"

"Don't scare me off now, Flo! The die is already cast, there's no going back. Cheerio." And with that, Jan hung up. Florence knew this was neither the time nor the place to tell her about Arthur. As Florence went to bed, however, her heart felt a little lighter, knowing that Jan's appearance in Arthur's classroom would be something for him to look forward to tomorrow.

Chapter Fifteen

Pirates!

THE NEXT MORNING DAWNED BRIGHT AND COLD. At the Bannister Elementary School the staff room was busy with teachers grabbing a last cup of coffee before class, photocopying activity sheets, and checking mailboxes. There were no students in the hallways just yet. The intercom buzzed to life: "Miss Mitchell, you have a call on line one, Miss Mitchell."

Miss Mitchell picked up the phone inside her classroom and pressed the flashing red button.

"This is Miss Mitchell, how can I help you?" It was Florence on the other end, calling from the Fine Arts Centre.

"I am Florence Dunne calling again about Arthur. There was an incident yesterday after school. He was accosted by two students. He was pushed to the ground, and the contents of his backpack were thrown around."

"I'm so sorry, Ms. Dunne. Who were those students?" she asked.

"This is the problem," Florence admitted, "Arthur won't tell me their names for fear of reprisal. I'll ask you again to please keep an eye out for any suspicious activity. I know these things go underground, and they always happen at recess or when your back is turned. But if you notice anything at all, let me know immediately. I obviously don't want another incident like this to occur!" Florence said with feeling.

"Of course you don't Ms. Dunne. I will keep watch," she said with determination.

"Thanks so much. Let's keep in touch," Florence said and rang off.

Miss Mitchell sat down at her desk and put her head in her hands. She felt enormous guilt that Arthur had had to deal with such bullying. She cared for her students, but this group of children had proved to be challenging ever since September. There was more pressure on her because in the Bannister Bay area of Moorland in particular, the parents were mostly leaders in commerce. They had big plans for their children and expected them to be straight A students. If they didn't, the blame was placed on the teacher.

And there were a lot of boys in her class. She had spent the Christmas holidays planning lessons better geared to their active learning style. Her hard work had paid off for the most part. However, this period of time before spring break was the hardest. Teachers were taxed to their limit, and a holiday was long overdue for both instructors and students alike. Perhaps she had been ignoring small incidents that even two weeks ago she would have picked up on.

And then the bell rang.

After lunch recess Miss Mitchell's class came in as usual, but this time there was someone else chatting with their teacher. She was tall and wiry with closely cropped salt-and-pepper hair. She actually looked like a gym instructor because she was wearing a casual blue blouse, jeans, and sneakers. There was also a huge skull-and-cross-bones flag pinned to the front bulletin board that had definitely not been there for their morning classes.

"Class, I'd like you to meet Miss Clayton. She is an artist and worked at the Moorland Fine Arts Centre for many years as an art teacher," Miss Mitchell said. "Miss Clayton is going to help us with our art projects for this year's school musical. Please give her our warm grade three welcome."

The class got to their feet and said in sing-song unison, "Good afternoon Miss Clayton" and then sat back down. Jan Clayton faced the class, caught Arthur's eye, and gave him a big smile. Suddenly she grabbed what looked like a sword from the table behind her and brandished it above her head yelling,

"Argh, me hearties! Are you ready for some adventure?" She waved the sword above her head again. Then she laughed as she saw the amazed faces that looked up at her and put the sword tip down on the floor in front of her.

"Who am I?" she asked the students. By now Miss Mitchell had moved out of the way and was sitting where could see both the children and Miss Clayton. Many hands went up in response to the question, and a few "I knows" could be heard. Jan pointed to an enthusiastic boy towards the back of the room. It was Lance.

"You be a pirate," Lance said, standing up and delivering the line in a strong, exaggeratedly deep voice. The whole class laughed.

"That I be," said Jan in response. "And I'm asking you to come with me to a time when big ships ruled the waves and a pirate ship was to be feared."

The class began with Jan showing them all manner of pirate artifacts—replicas gathered from her many travels around the world with her sister Dorothy. The sword she brandished was wooden but painted in such a way as to appear real. Ancient gold coins, sextants, treasure maps, and a blunderbuss were all carefully passed around the room. Finally Jan started to pass out small sketchbooks and pencils to each one in the class.

"Imagine that you are part of the crew of a pirate ship. You are going to fly your pirate flag. What do you think you'd want on that flag?" Jan asked the class.

"A gun!" Greg yelled out. Unperturbed, Jan responded,

"A gun would be an excellent choice. Just remember that every image you use must be something from long ago. Are there any other ideas?" she asked the class.

"Miss Clayton, were girls pirates?" asked a student.

"Of course they were! They had to disguise themselves, although some accounts say that they only did that when they were fighting!" Jan smiled.

"By the way, class, I came early and plundered your library of all its pirate books. They're on the table at the front of the room. Miss Mitchell has made a sign-up sheet for each book. And these sketchbooks that I've handed out are for you to put all your ideas in. We have a lot of projects for this musical!"

"Can we use our sketchbooks now?" Addison asked.

"Of course you may. Please come up with at least three different ideas for your flag design," Jan added. She proceeded to walk up and down the aisles answering more questions and commenting on the sketches the students were doing. She tried not to spend too much time chatting with Arthur because she didn't want to leave out any of the other children.

By the end of the class, each child had at least one design drawn. The sketchbooks were gathered up, and Jan had put her pirate treasures back in the weathered chest that she had brought.

"Thank you, grade three, for welcoming me into your classroom," she said. "I will leave my Jolly Roger and my pirate chest with you. I'm sure Miss Mitchell will take care of it." So saying, she lay the chest down on the table.

"What about the sword?" asked Henry.

"This sword stays with me. It's travelled the high seas and is even older than I am, so it needs to go home and rest." She left the classroom, waving as she went, with a quick wink to Arthur.

"Is she your friend?" Seymour asked, leaning over and whispering to Arthur.

"Yes," Arthur whispered back.

"Cool," Seymour said.

Chapter Sixteen

Before the Concert

THE REST OF THE WEEK PASSED WITHOUT INCIDENT for Arthur. Perhaps it was because word got out that he was a friend of Miss Clayton, or it could have been that the class was caught up in their pirate flag project. Miss Mitchell gave them thirty minutes at the end of each day to research and draw, though she had to remind a few students that machine guns were not historically accurate images for an ancient flag.

One day at the end of that week, she came into her classroom to find the pirate chest opened. She quickly checked the contents but determined that nothing was missing. She made a note to herself to check the door to make sure it was locked before she left for lunch. She had thought a great deal about the personalities in her room and worried that she should have been firmer with a few individuals. Right now she had no proof, just suspicions about who could be bullying Arthur. It was illuminating not only to watch Jan teach, but to observe her students in the learning process.

On Friday, Florence, Bucket, and Arthur prepared for the spring concert of the Moorland Children's Choir. Arthur was still talking about his school's pirate project and Jan's visit to the classroom. Bucket was enthusing about her musical rehearsals and humming "Climbing Over Rocky Mountain" as she got ready. Florence had completed her new application form for graduate studies at the University of Moorland and dropped it off right after work. Even the dog was full of energy when they had taken her for a quick walk in the park—fetching and herding the family back and forth. All was right with the world.

The choir uniform was simply black pants or skirt and a white shirt. The accent was a red ascot for the girls and a red bow tie for the boys. Bucket liked to do her own hair, which was a shoulder-length chestnut brown with a natural wave that tended to bounce out in its own direction. Arthur's wispy blond locks were easy to train with just a bit of water and a comb. Shoes, however, needed touch-ups at the last minute. Florence kept on her work clothes to simplify the procedure. Finally they were ready. Florence bent down and talked to Presto.

"We're going to be gone for a few hours. You be good, Presto. Stay and look after the house." She gave her a final pat before closing the door behind them.

"Miss Mitchell says Jan is coming next week," Arthur told his mother as he buckled himself in.

"Yes, she phoned me at work and told me. She said you have a lot of projects to do and you've gotten a head start by getting something done before spring break."

"Gosh, Arthur, you're lucky doing the art-work. Mr. Harbicht hardly ever lets us do art. Maybe once a week for a reward," Bucket complained.

"Well, it said in the school newsletter that Mr. Harbicht and a team of parents are going to create the flats for the backdrop," her mother countered.

"Well, I hope the parents have fun!" Bucket said grumpily.

"Brigitte Ethel Boisvert, don't ever use that tone of voice with me, young lady. You have one of the biggest roles in the musical. You are privileged to have teachers willing to go above and beyond to produce this show." Florence raised her voice in her anger, something that rarely happened. She also never used Bucket's full name unless she was extremely upset.

"Sorry Mom. I know I'm lucky," Bucket said apologetically. "Really I do."

There was silence in the moving car. Florence already regretted her outburst and looked in the rear-view mirror to see Bucket with her head down.

"Everyone's talking about the musical. Lance wants to start a pirate club," Arthur said, cutting through the quiet. "We're going to paint the flags next week. I've got tons of ideas," he enthused. "It's gonna be a surprise!"

"Rowena's mom called me about doing some sewing for the costumes. And we'll spend some time over the holiday, Bucket, looking for a few things I know you'll need," their mother said, calm now and wanting to reconnect with her daughter.

As she dropped off the children at the stage door, she waved to Diane Black, who was shepherding all the children down to the rehearsal area behind the stage. Parking the car, Florence felt she could do with a bit more time before the concert began. The concert hall was a part of the performing arts complex on the University of Moorland campus. The building was funded by generous benefactors. It was clear the main thrust of the university was science, so anything of an artistic nature was always privately financed.

Florence went to the student centre and bought a cappuccino to go. She leisurely walked around the buildings and flower beds, noticing what perennials were starting to show signs of life. There was construction around the library. She had read that even though the university was young, it aspired to be a leader in engineering. Moorland itself was experiencing a boom, so it was natural that the community would want a flagship educational institution as well. That would be good for Bucket and Arthur because they would certainly benefit once they had finished high school. If they went into the sciences it would be even better. There was no predicting what the coming eight or nine years would reveal for each of her children. Bucket seemed determined to become a vet, while Arthur had always been fascinated by flight.

As Florence walked about, identifying the different buildings, she thought about being a student again. She could imagine doing just what she was doing at this moment—taking life at a much more leisurely pace. An image in her mind grew of herself wearing blue jeans every day; walking to class; talking to young people; volunteering in the children's classrooms; getting home early and making a complex, gourmet dinner; swimming with Bucket and Arthur on the week-ends—Florence shook her head. There would still be papers to write, deadlines to meet, bells that rang. The big difference would be that she was really on her own time. She could skip class if she wanted to. The thought made her shiver. In all the years she had worked at the Fine Arts Centre she had missed a total of two weeks of work. What was certain, was that it would be a complete change of pace from the years of doing what she had been doing. Florence was ready for a change.

Chapter Seventeen

Songs Around the World

In the concert hall, Florence found that she had stayed too long outside enjoying the spring weather: there was only space for her to sit on the far left at the back. It didn't matter. An aisle seat gave her the opportunity to get an unobstructed view of the piano and Carey Biggs, the accompanist. Carey was such a showman and played to the audience's appreciation of his expressive musicianship. His piano playing was emotive, while his whole body bent into each piece, and his shoulders moved with each subtle nuance of the music. He always kept a watchful eye on the conductor, whether it was Mrs. Cauldwell or Ms. Moster. Sometimes his hands would be poised expectantly above the keyboard waiting for the signal to begin playing.

Mrs. Cauldwell, dressed in a full-length black sequined ball gown, gave the opening remarks.

"Welcome one and all, and thank you for coming out this evening. The children have been working hard since Christmas to put together our spring concert titled—'Songs Around The World'. They've learned to sing in Japanese, German, Xhosa, Zulu and Afrikaans. Please welcome Ms. Moster, who will conduct our opening numbers." She gestured to the wings, and Ms. Moster walked out followed by the Moorland Children's Choir marching in single file.

They ascended the risers that seemed to fill the large stage. Bucket was between her two friends Rowena and Providence, or Ro and Pro, as she called them. Florence noted that the girls had done up their hair in matching pony tails with red ribbons. She smiled at the evidence of their friendship. Then Lance and Arthur came in the second row. She noticed that they were not standing together, and she was sure she knew why. There were two girls in between them. Arthur's bow-tie looked a little crooked. He had a serious expression on his face and held his arms straight at his sides when he faced the conductor.

Ms. Moster, in a simple black sheath, organized the rows, making sure each chorister could see her. Then she turned to the audience.

"Our first number this evening will be 'Sakura, Sakura' sung in Japanese. It is a song depicting spring in Japan, 'sakura' meaning cherry blossoms," Ms. Moser said in her clear, emphatic voice.

And so the concert began. Florence sometimes sat back, closed her eyes, and just listened to the beautiful music. At other times she watched the children, the accompanist, and the conductor. Mrs. Cauldwell had started the choir to give Moorland a much-needed place for its children to learn choral music. She had high standards for what children could achieve. Her expectations pervaded the organization, from the kind of discipline she expected to the difficulty of the music she wanted them to learn. Ms. Moster was in her second year with the organization, a young woman in her last year of education program at the university. She was very professional, but not in the same all-commanding style of Mrs. Cauldwell.

Other choirs had sprung up in Moorland over the years, but

Mrs. Cauldwell's was the very first. Some organizations offered children a chance to dance with their singing, making it more like musical theatre. Their performances always had costumes and big production numbers. But the Moorland Children's Choir had maintained its focus, even though some of its members left for what they saw as a more exciting time. Mrs. Cauldwell, as artistic director of the choir, was adamant that musicianship not be sacrificed for glitz. Parents who enrolled their kids in the choir agreed and felt they were paying for a top-notch musical education. Florence concurred, but Bucket and Arthur had begun their choir experience not because of the choir's philosophy, but because their rehearsals were only two blocks away from the first house they lived in. Now it was a bit of a drive, but everyone agreed that it was well worth it.

After Bucket and Arthur's group sang, they went off stage and were replaced by the littlest group, the Moorland Junior Children's Choir. Florence always looked forward to their set. Even their entrances and exits were delightful to watch. She knew that the youngest was five years old. They were all either in kindergarten or grade one. They were going to sing 'Margery Maketh the Tea,' a song Florence had never heard before. Mrs. Cauldwell, who always conducted this group, led them around the risers right to the front of the stage. Then she stood just below them, off the stage, so the little people could be seen. Mrs. Cauldwell turned to the audience and said,

"Now children, wave to your mommies and daddies," where upon they waved vigorously at the crowd, some shielding their eyes from the bright stage lights. The audience laughed. They were well used to this technique. Once the waves were out of the way, the children could be persuaded to sing their song.

For this song Mrs. Cauldwell had added gestures. The tiny choir watched her carefully, making sure they got the right action for the right word. However, there was one little girl on the far left at the end of the row, who Florence could see was just that much behind in her timing. When the group were led off stage, this little girl stood gazing absently out into the audience while swishing her skirt with her arms. Then she suddenly jumped up and yelled out, "Daddy!" and ran down the steps and out into the audience. The crowd roared its approval.

The concert continued with numbers from the Moorland Youth Choir. They were choristers who were out of high school, but still wanted the choral experience. Their repertoire was that much more difficult, but it was also peppered with jazz standards and pop tunes to keep up interest. Florence enjoyed this choir because it gave her a glimpse into some of the possibilities for Bucket and Arthur in the future. She also delighted in seeing how the kids had grown. Her family had been with the organization for five years, so she had seen some of the youth singers since they were about Arthur's age. Looking at them, she reflected that you never knew how your children would turn out. There were hopes and dreams, but, as she knew all too well, life could take U-turns.

Just before the last number, Mrs. Cauldwell came back on stage for her closing remarks. She was smiling as she elegantly walked to the microphone.

"Again, parents, relatives and friends—and all the supporters of the Moorland Children's Choir—thank you so much for attending 'Songs Around the World'. We hope you have enjoyed your journey. And speaking of journeys, parents don't forget that next year is our tour year. We are certainly excited about it and hope that you are too. Please send in those forms before the end of May so we can get an indication of how many children are planning to go. Good night everyone. Please stay for treats in the foyer." She walked to the front of the massed choir while Ms. Moster joined the sopranos.

They sang 'N'Kosi Sikelel' 'i Africa', the stirring South African anthem. With all the children singing together, it had an innocent quality. The young men who were bass in the youth section of the choir definitely shone in this beautiful piece of music. Florence wondered when Arthur's voice would change. She hoped that day was a long way off because his boy's soprano seemed a bit higher than Bucket's at the moment. Their rendition of this moving anthem brought the concert to a resounding conclusion. It made Florence wonder how the choirs could top this for their final presentation in June.

As usual after a concert it was hard to make a quick getaway. Bucket and Arthur were enjoying their well-earned snacks and drinks, while Florence caught up with a few parents and Diane Black. There was a big display of the tour placed strategically near the coffee table. There were colourful brochures showing all the venues for the choir's various concerts, and places where they would be touring. It was all very impressive, with a detailed itinerary spelled out. There was also the price per chorister, in small typeface, on the back of the glossy brochure parents could take home. Florence stood rooted to the spot as she looked at the number. She told herself to buck up as she quietly pocketed the brochure. After all, it was over a year away, although they wanted a preliminary payment before the end of the school year.

On the way home, Florence quietly asked,

"Are any of your friends talking about the tour?"

"Oh yes, mom," Bucket said. "Both Ro and Pro want to go, but their parents haven't decided yet."

"Lance is going," Arthur affirmed. "His dad already said. They're gonna plan a holiday right after the tour."

"That sounds exciting. We've never been to Europe, Mom," Bucket stated.

"I know. It does sound exciting to go to the United Kingdom. Both of your grandparents came from England, you know. We could even visit where they were born." Florence was starting to get caught up in the prospect of an exotic family holiday, in spite of herself.

"Don't forget,"Arthur reminded her. "We always go with Dad to the lake in the summer."

"That's true," his mother said, "but not for the whole time. We've got lots to think about, don't we?"

"Gee, Mom! It would be so much fun. Arthur and I have never been on tour," Bucket said thoughtfully.

"It would certainly be an educational experience." That made both Florence's children groan, and then they burst out laughing. They were used to their mother always pointing out the greater educational value of their extra-curricular activities. She joined in the laughter too, cheered that her children didn't take her seriously all of the time. And as they drove out of the parking garage on their way back home, Florence thought that maybe being a student again in the coming year would allow her the luxury of loosening up on her own onerous sense of responsibility.

Chapter Eighteen

The Weekend—Gone in a Flash

SATURDAY AND SUNDAY PASSED QUICKLY FOR THE FAMILY. It was Florence's week-end for the children. Lance came over on Saturday afternoon to play with Arthur. The boys set about making pirate eye patches out of some scrap pieces of leather Florence happened to have in her box of sewing supplies. Lance, a single child, was always happy to spend time at Florence's home with her menagerie of two kids and a dog.

Providence came over the same afternoon to be with Bucket. The two girls practised their lines for *The Pirates of Penzance*. Florence picked out the melody of their songs on the piano. For supper, Florence cut up vegetables, cheese, and pepperoni. The children had their own pizza rounds, so they could make their own, just the way they liked it. Around the dinner table there was plenty of talk about the choir tour. Florence hung back and let the kids talk. She was still calculating how she would be able to afford the two children's travel fees. Her ex-husband had started up a new business and a new family. There was no largesse coming from that quarter that could possibly offset the tour costs.

Sunday disappeared in a blur of church-going, taking the dog for a long walk in the park, and doing homework. Florence never liked to have the day before work and school to be too crowded. Spring was in the air, and being outside gave everyone glowing cheeks and a good appetite for dinner. That evening Florence again contemplated her options for the coming year. She was so hopeful for her admission to the University of Moorland. Studying under Anna Sexton also had a definite appeal, but that would mean uprooting her family and moving out of province. Whether absence for an extended period of time was even allowed by the divorce agreement, she had no idea.

In the eyes of the law, Florence had full custody. According to the divorce document, Jean and Marie had the children live with them on alternate weekends. This usually involved just Saturday night, depending on Bucket's and Arthur's activities. In the beginning of their separation and then divorce, times away from the children yawned like an empty chasm for Florence. But now, after five years of this arrangement, she had become adept at planning things to do that she knew the kids wouldn't necessarily enjoy. All of her close friends were married with children and were not negligent in including her in their own lives. However, Florence didn't want to become a third wheel in any case, so she became industrious on her own. The house always needed cleaning up, maintenance, and repairs, which she tried schooling herself to do. Her biggest triumph was installing a dining room fixture. It had taken a few trips to the hardware store and some friendly advice from one of the clerks, but she did it on her own without being electrocuted.

As Florence went to bed that night she worried about the coming year. What initially had seemed like such an amazing gift held within it the unknown. She thought of one of her professors who had talked about a "treasure burden." This was a gift that contained hidden difficulties, not obvious in the initial reception of the present. Florence was beginning to feel that her sabbatical year was one such a gift. She had not told her ex-husband that she had even received a sabbatical. She reasoned that at the moment they were all still living within the status quo.

Chapter Nineteen

Pirate Club

IT WAS THE WEEK BEFORE SPRING BREAK. At Wednesday morning recess, Arthur and his friends were enjoying their game of pirates. It had started out on Monday, just with Lance. But now Addison, Seymour, and their new friend Lau were all a part of the fun. Each night Arthur made more eye patches to accommodate the new inductees. They had on their eye patches now and were in a huddle in the middle of the playground. It was a bright, clear spring day.

"Hey, Arthur," Addison said, "let's pretend there's treasure in the playground somewhere."

"I know, I know!" Lance said with enthusiasm. "We could make a treasure map."

"Yeah," Seymour said, "I bet I know who could draw it—Lau."

"Sure," responded Lau, shyly. He and his sister, Chim, had recently arrived at the school. Everyone in Miss Mitchell's class had noticed that Lau was a good artist. His drawings were always detailed and skilful.

"C'mon. Let's see if we can find a good hiding place for the treasure!" Arthur cried. All the boys put on their eye patches and with a collective, "Aaargh!" ran off with Addison in the lead. They followed him behind a clump of bushes at the far end of the playground.

"Would this be good?" Addison asked, out of breath.

"Nah, you could see it from the road," Lance gestured to the street on the other side of the chain-link fence.

"Maybe," Seymour said, unsure.

"Maybe you guys are just losers!" Greg shouted, accosting them from the other side of the bushes. Henry was close on his heels along with a couple of grade two students.

"What's your problem?" Lance challenged, standing in front of Greg.

"I just wanna be a pirate like you guys, honest," Greg said, changing tack.

"I bet," Arthur said under his breath.

"Can I try out the eye patch, huh?" Greg asked with a smirk.

"I'd like to try one!" Henry said with evident interest. One of the grade two students nodded his head in agreement.

"All right, you can try mine, Henry," Seymour said. He carefully took off his eye patch and gave it to Henry. Henry put it on and turned to show the other kids.

"Well, where's mine?" Greg demanded. Addison reluctantly took his off and passed it to Greg. As soon as Greg grabbed the eye patch, he pulled at it, causing the sewing to give way and ripping it into two uneven pieces.

"Hey, what'd you do that for?" Addison cried, moving toward Greg. Greg just laughed and ran away, with Henry and the others stumbling after him. Henry tore off his eye patch as he went, letting it fall on the ground behind him.

"That guy is ridiculous!" Seymour said, picking up the pieces of Addison's eye patch.

"Give it to me," Arthur said resignedly, "I can fix it for you, Add."

"What's his problem?" Lau asked, who hadn't encountered Greg's bullying before.

"Who knows?" Addison said in exasperation.

"And who cares!" Lance added emphatically.

The school bell rang to signal the end of recess. As the boys walked back to the school, they retrieved Seymour's eye patch.

"What about the treasure map?" Seymour asked, wanting to continue their game of pirates.

"Yeah, we gotta do that," Lance agreed,

"Recess, tomorrow!" Addison stated.

"Argh!" they all yelled in unison and laughed, relieved to be moving forward. Stuffing their eye patches in their pockets, they walked into the school. Arthur, following his friends into the hallway, cheered up, at least momentarily. He decided that he would have a new eye patch for Addison ready for tomorrow's recess. After that it was the holidays and everyone would be gone.

Chapter Twenty

What Now?

On that same Wednesday, as the afternoon rolled around, Florence started to believe that there was a light at the end of the tunnel. She would be getting off at noon on Friday. The Centre classes were done for the day, and most of the staff had already disappeared. But she wanted to make sure her plans were secure for tomorrow's last day of teaching for the term, as well as the week following the holiday. Florence liked the security of having her classes organized well in advance. There would always be changes, especially teaching at the Centre, because she never knew what the students would be like until they walked through the drama room door.

"You shouldn't always be the last one to leave," Carole teased.

"Bucket has a rehearsal after school, so I've still got a bit of time. What have you got planned for the break, Carole?" Florence asked, as she leaned on Carole's double pedestal antique oak desk.

"Actually we're all going to Disneyland! We're leaving bright and early Saturday morning, with the hordes of other families, I'm sure," Carole said as she started to tidy up the papers on her desk.

"I don't know how you've kept your trip secret in this staff room."

"You know me...I like to have every t crossed and i dotted before I say anything. Actually it was one of those last-minute deals. I just happened to drop in to my travel agency, and there it was! So I seized the day, as Jan used to always tell us to do. And you're the first to know about my plans." She got up and gave Florence a big hug.

"Let me guess—now you're going home to pack!" Florence exclaimed.

"Absolutely! See you tomorrow Flo," Carole said, giving a little wave as she left the staff room. Just then the phone rang. It sounded shrill and demanding in the quiet room. Florence reached over Carole's desk and picked it up.

"May I speak to Ms. Florence Dunne, please?" the voice said.

"Yes, I'm Florence," she said as she walked around and sat in Carole's chair. She picked up a pen and note-pad, thinking she might have to record something.

"This is Mrs. Melling from the Department of Education at the University of Moorland," she said in an officious manner. Florence wrote down just what she had told her.

"This is in regards to your application for graduate studies," Mrs. Melling continued.

"Yes?" Florence asked hopefully, her heart starting to beat quickly and her palms beginning to perspire.

"There was some confusion with your re-application. I presume you know we have both on file?" Mrs. Melling said in a condescending tone.

"Yes, I expect you would," Florence said, gulping.

"We have a quota on fine arts graduate students in either the education or arts faculties," intoned Mrs. Melling.

"I certainly wasn't aware of that," Florence said, starting to feel a little sick to her stomach.

"What I'm trying to tell you dear, is that the quota was reached in both faculties." Florence had no response. Mrs. Melling continued as if to fill in the gap. "You do realize your applications were received towards the last possible date for submission?"

"Yes I knew. But I had only just received confirmation of my sabbatical," Florence protested.

"Really, Ms. Dunne, that's certainly not our affair," Mrs. Melling responded, clearing her throat. "The department head asked me to call you, so you may expedite an application elsewhere."

"That's very considerate of you," Florence said testily and hung up the phone before Mrs. Melling had a chance to tell her what else she had done wrong.

Florence sat at Carole's desk, making swirls and doodles around the words she had written on the memo pad. She wasn't even aware of what she was doing. She was deadened somehow by the news. Her mind was a blank. She was drifting around in some plane of existence that was nowhere near the staff room of the Moorland Fine Arts Centre.

She thought about the hopes and dreams she had for her little family. They had moved into their own home three years ago. They all loved its many windows, its old hardwood floors and funny double-long closets. The neighbourhood wasn't too far away from Bucket and Arthur's school and other activities, and she could afford it. There was a wonderful off-leash park two blocks away for Presto's walks. She had bought the house all by herself in the wake of her divorce. The children each had their own room, something they had never had before. It was a beautiful spot. That dream had been realized.

Now another dream grew in its place. Florence wanted to get her master's degree. Being at the Fine Arts Centre had made her want to take her teaching to the next level, to challenge herself and her students. At the Centre she taught in front of teachers every day, so she had become acutely aware of her teaching methodology. She really wanted to study drama-in-education in a profound way so that she could bring a deeper understanding to her work at the Centre.

Florence thought that becoming a student again would be a challenge in itself. In addition, it might be exhilarating to be the recipient of knowledge rather than the purveyor of it. The year would be an opportunity to open up her mind to other worlds of understanding and thought. She would have time to let her mind wander, the way it was wandering now. As of this moment, Florence had to face the fact that her sabbatical would never be at the Moorland University. Where was she going to go? What was she going to do? How could she possibly even entertain the thought of uprooting her family?

With a start, Florence noticed that the time had been ticking away while she had been day-dreaming. The memo pad was filled with squiggles, most of them crisscrossing over Mrs. Melling's name. It wasn't her fault. She was just the messenger, Florence realized. She crumpled up the paper and threw it away. She went to her own desk to pick up her briefcase and jacket and she strode out the staff rooms door without a backward glance.

Chapter Twenty-One

Pirate Rehearsal

By the time Florence drove up to the school, the reality of her situation was beginning to dawn. She tried not to panic, but a building sense of unease was causing her stomach to do butterfly flips. She took a deep breath and went into the school.

She could hear them practising as soon as she stepped into the front hall. The girl's chorus was singing "Climbing Over Rocky Mountain". To Florence's sympathetic ear, they sounded quite wonderful. There was no one in the hallway, so she tiptoed to the gymnasium, hoping to catch a bit of the rehearsal.

As she edged through the doorway she noticed Arthur sitting on the gym floor with his nose in the big UFO book he had renewed yet again from the library. To Florence, his curiosity about extra-terrestrial life was a natural extension of his obsession with anything related to science. She herself, along with a close cousin of hers, had been fascinated by flying saucers. For many years she borrowed library books about the subject and read science fiction voraciously. Arthur caught onto her interest in UFOs and was always quizzing her about the Dunne's family stories concerning the saucers.

Then she saw Bucket on stage with the rest of the girl's chorus. Ms.

Moster was talking to them quietly, and they were paging through their musical scores. Mrs. Cauldwell had many responsibilities other than music teaching at Bannister Elementary and being the artistic director of the Moorland Children's Choir. She was on many boards of performing arts organizations throughout the city. She was occasionally out at meetings. In the past two years, she had prevailed upon Ms. Moster to pinch-hit for her. Nobody minded.

"Alright girls," she said. "We don't have the pirates here, but I'd like to try "Poor Wand'ring One" with a little bit of blocking, just so we get the idea." Everyone clustered in the middle of the stag, and looked out at Ms. Moster eagerly. She was just below the stage, by the piano, angled so that there was a direct line of sight between her and the children.

"Mabel—I mean Bucket—when you start to sing your solo, try stepping away from your sisters so that you are more downstage. Pretend you are singing to Frederick." At this last remark, Florence could see Providence nudge a few of the girls standing next to her. Bucket just smiled. They had put some stage lights on, so Florence could see everyone clearly, but she herself remained in shadow at the back of the gym. Arthur looked up to the stage now and then but he seemed mainly involved in reading his book.

"OK, ladies," Ms. Moster smiled. "Here's your two-bar intro: one, two, three; one, two, three. Poor wand'ring one," she sang with the chorus and played the piano accompaniment. When it came to Mabel's first solo section, Bucket put down her score, stepped out, and swayed with the music as she sang. When it came to her second solo, she moved left and right in the waltz rhythm of the music. By the time Ms. Moster played her last solo part, Bucket mimed waltzing with an imaginary partner swirling around the stage. All the girls clapped and laughed at Bucket when the song was over. Arthur noticed and he was laughing too.

Florence knew that Bucket was studious and attacked everything with zeal, but she hadn't realized that her daughter had memorized this particular number so quickly. Observing Bucket from the sidelines like this was a revelation for Florence. With a shock she saw Bucket, although only ten years old, as a young lady now, with an emerging vibrant personality. There she was, up on stage, her very own person. Why had this never dawned on Florence before? Of course, the transition from child to person-hood was a process and didn't happen overnight. For so long Florence had been bound up in her role as a mother/protector/nurturer that she hadn't realized what was going on under her own nose.

The rehearsal continued. Ms. Moster was asking Bucket to sing some additional notes for the third solo in the song. She sang the part while playing it on the piano and then Bucket echoed the notes. It was like an arpeggio going higher and higher from the last note of her solo. Florence had no idea that Bucket could sing in that descant range. It was another surprise.

The girls came down from the stage and crowded around the piano, all wanting to try the higher notes. It seemed only Bucket could manage the intricacies of the high soprano part. Ms. Moster good-naturedly gave everyone a chance and finally told them that the rehearsal was over.

"Mrs. Cauldwell is certainly lucky to have such an enthusiastic group of singers," Ms. Moster told them as they were packing up, getting ready to go.

"Hi Mom!" Bucket said as she noticed her Mother walking towards them.

"Hi dear," Florence answered. "Thanks for working with the kids," she said to Ms. Moster.

"It is my absolute pleasure," Ms. Moster responded, and she seemed to mean it. "Before you all go, don't forget to practice your music over the holidays. There won't be any rehearsal now for two whole weeks!"

As the girls slowly left the gym, chatting in small groups, Florence called to her son,

"Come on Arthur. We'd better not hold up Ms. Moster. I'm sure she has better things to do!"

"Actually he's been a big help," Ms. Moster countered. "He ran off some music that I needed, and the rest of the time he's just been reading. It must be a good book," she added.

"It sure is," Arthur replied. "Mom, can I show you something before we leave?"

"If it's just a minute, I think they're closing up the school," his mother said. After saying good-bye to Ms. Moster, Arthur led them down the hallway to the art room. Mr. Gizo had told Arthur he would leave the door open for him.

"Look, mom," said Arthur. "We painted our pirate flags this afternoon!" He turned on the light, and there, drying out on the tables were twenty different Jolly Rogers.

"Wow! You guys did awesome," said Bucket.

"Guess which one is mine," Arthur challenged them. All twenty flags were made from black cloth. Some flags had the recognizable skull and cross-bones painted in white. Others had chosen crossed swords and one had crossed old-style pistols. Bucket and her mother walked up and down the tables.

"I think I've got it, Arthur," Florence said triumphantly. "You're this one." She pointed to a flag with a red hourglass and white wings. The wings looked as if they were joined at the mid-point of the timekeeper.

"How did you know?" Arthur asked with real curiosity.

"Because,"—Bucket jumped in—"you're the only flag with wings on it. You love anything to do with flight. It was obvious, bro." Bucket gave her brother a friendly hug.

"Gee, I thought I was more mysterious than that!" Arthur said, but he smiled anyway.

"Altogether this looks pretty impressive. I'll bet they'll look great on stage," his mother commented.

"Yeah, I might even have to be afraid of those pirates," Bucket said with a chuckle.

Arthur turned out the lights and they left the room.

"Miss Mitchell says we get to put another coat of paint on them tomorrow morning," said Arthur. "She's going to iron the wrinkles out too. But it takes a long time to dry...maybe after the holidays," he added as they walked out of the school.

By the time they got home, everyone was hungry. Florence tried to feed her children only healthy food. At home there were never any soft drinks or junk food. Her one concession was popcorn, which she could happily have eaten any day of the week. Tonight Florence had a lot on her mind. Sometimes Bucket and Arthur would help with meal preparation, but Florence thought that it was a better use of their time to do homework and get that done and out of the way. As she surveyed the contents of her fridge and cupboards, she felt too distracted to be inspired to make anything fancy.

She settled on macaroni and cheese out of the box she got from her local health food store. It was a throw-back to when the children were little, but it would just have to do. The noodles were in shapes of bunnies and carrots. The writing on the package assured her that there were no additives or preservatives and that there was actual cheese used in the packet of orange powder. What a relief! With the addition of carrot sticks and fruit for dessert, Florence had just about ticked off all the items on the Canada Food Guide.

Chapter Twenty-Two

A Walk in the Park Worth Remembering

AFTER SUPPER, WHICH WAS WARMLY RECEIVED by Bucket and Arthur, they took Presto for a walk. The days were growing longer, and they all needed to get out and exercise. The park meandered by a stream with a small pond in the middle. There were bridges that crossed the stream in at least four strategic spots. An extended or short walk was possible depending on one's mood and the weather. The evening was becoming cool as the evening shadows grew longer.

Bucket and Arthur rode their bikes while their mother walked and jogged. She had the leash for Presto, just in case they needed it. Sometimes Florence would see a rabbit ahead and know that the dog would want to give chase. She'd quickly put on the leash, which saved her a vigorous run later on. Tonight she let the children ride ahead with Presto. She walked by the stream and tried to just enjoy the beautiful spring evening. There was no point stewing about the Moorland University rejection. She would have to take action and determine a different direction. Somehow it felt like another mountain she'd have to climb.

"Stop feeling sorry for yourself!" she muttered under her breath. She looked up and couldn't see Bucket or Arthur, or the dog.

Florence shook herself and jogged off, looking for the trio. She ran across one of the first bridges she knew they would cross. There was still no sign of them, so she continued her search, going a little slower to make sure she looked in all of the side pathways and clumps of trees. She turned a corner that took her to the base of the tallest hill in the park and stopped. There in front of her were the two children crouching down with Presto in between them. Their bikes were lying on the side of the pathway, and they were looking up to the top of the hill.

"Mom, look up there," Bucket whispered.

Florence moved quietly and quickly to stand behind them. She could hardly believe her eyes. On top of the hill was a coyote, calmly looking down at them. The animal appeared to be giving them the once-over.

"We thought he was a dog, mom," Arthur whispered.

"He sure looks like a dog—but he's not!" their mother whispered back. The coyote held his head up high and seemed to be sniffing the air. Then he turned and melted away.

"Whew," breathed Bucket.

"We weren't scared," Arthur said. "We just didn't want Presto to get hurt!"

"You did right Arthur," their mother confirmed. "There could be members of his pack on the other side of the hill." She got out the leash and put it on the dog.

"Let's go back by the little bridge," she said.

They retraced their steps and then took a different route over an old stone bridge to make their journey shorter. Bucket and Arthur walked their bikes while their mother held Presto tight by her side on the leash. They kept an eye out for any coyotes, but they didn't see one again.

"Would the coyote hurt us, Mom?" Arthur asked.

"I really don't think so," his mother said. "It's unusual to see wildlife in this area. It must have come up the Arrow River somehow."

"He was a beautiful animal, wasn't he?" Bucket stated.

"Aw, you're such an animal lover!" Arthur teased.

"It was actually a treat to see the coyote, wasn't it?" their Mother said. "But we'll have to keep Presto on a leash until it moves out of the area."

"What about other people?" Arthur asked, worried.

"Actually you're right," their mother said. "We should really warn other dog owners that there's a coyote in the area."

"I know mom. We could make a sign and hang it up on the fence at the beginning of the park," Bucket said.

"Now that's an excellent idea. You and Arthur can do that as soon as we get home."

Presto led the way homeward tugging on the leash. As soon as they were a few blocks away, the dog always surged forward, eager for treats and a bowl of water. She hadn't been afraid of the coyote—more curious than anything.

Back home Florence found a big piece of cardboard she cut out of a box that was storing their winter boots. Arthur and Bucket used permanent black marker to create the sign which read: WARNING! COYOTE IN PARK!! SPOTTED APRIL 12!!! Arthur had the idea to cover it in packing tape so it would weather the rain predicted for Easter. Their mother hole-punched the corners and threaded pieces of nylon cord through each. The children took the finished sign down to the trail head going into the park. There was a chain-link fence there, and they could tie the sign right to the fence. Presto went with them, trotting along beside Bucket who had the dog leashed.

As Florence cleared up, she realized she hadn't heard from her sister for a while. She had just assumed Edie and Wilt would be with them for Easter dinner. She wanted to go shopping while the children were in choir practice tomorrow, so it was important to know if she should buy a big turkey, little ham, or both. As Florence watched the children from the dining room window, she telephoned her sister.

"Hello," Edie said in an unusually soft voice.

"Hi, Edie, it's me your ever-loving sis," said Florence with a cheer she was not really feeling. But Edie didn't sound like her usual high-powered self, so Florence couldn't be a sad sack as well. It would make for a very miserable conversation.

"Of course, I know it's you!" Edie said with some annoyance.

"That's a relief," said Florence with a laugh. "Are you and Wilt still up for the long drive to Moorland? I'm going to be buying all the goodies for the week-end tomorrow. I'm determined this year to beat the rush."

"That's just it, Flo," said Edie with some hesitation. "We won't be coming."

"Hey, I thought you had it all worked out this time, Edie," Florence said with some consternation. She had really been looking forward to their visit. Wilt immersed himself in the Moorland archives, which gave her and her sister lots of time to visit and do special activities with Bucket and Arthur.

"You know what it's like. Wilt's business can run without him for a few days, but one of his assistant managers took sick and has pneumonia. He was even in the hospital this week with it, so Wilt's got to pick up the slack." Edie sounded resigned.

"Well, that's two less mouths to feed," said Florence, trying to make light of it. But her heart sank anyway.

"How's the graduate app going, Flo?" Edie asked, changing the subject.

"No go, I'm afraid," Florence sighed. "There was something about a quota for a masters in the fine arts. Who knew?"

"That's ridiculous and you know it! You should rattle a few cages up there and get them to see sense!" Edie stormed, sounding like her old self again.

"I'm afraid it's a done deal. Now I have to go to plan B. Except that I don't have a plan B just yet."

"What about Anna Saxton's University? I thought you were looking into their programs already?"

"Kinda, sorta. Maybe that's what I'll do with all the time I'll have this holiday. I've got nothing better to do!"

"OK, Rub it in! My hands were tied with this decision!"

Florence almost said, "They always are," but caught herself in time. Wilt's business had always been the priority in their household even though Edie held down a very responsible position as head secretary in one of the biggest law firms in the province. Edie's firm handled many of the native land claim's cases. These were always complex legal undertakings. Edie was one of their most prized employees because she had a grasp of the issues involved going back fifteen years. She was their most senior member as well, and each lawyer knew they could rely on her expertise implicitly.

"We saw a coyote in the park Edie," Florence said instead, not wanting to discuss her academic problems.

"You must be kidding!" Edie exclaimed.

"No, it was sitting on top of the big hill, as bold as brass. The kids just went out to put up a warning sign. It's an off-leash area, so any little dog would be fair game for those jaws. Even so, it was quite a sight."

"Now listen to me Flo," Edie said with determination. "Get going on that grant application. You deserve to get accepted into graduate school. You'd die of boredom just taking three random classes next year. And besides, it wouldn't move you up the pay scale either."

"Oh sorry, Edie, I've got to go. The kids are coming up the back walk, and I locked the door," Florence said in a nervous rush of words.

"You call me over the holiday OK?" Edie said, not wanting to be cut off.

"OK, sis. Love you," Florence said hastily.

"Love you too," Edie said and hung up.

As Florence turned towards the back-door, she noticed the vividness of the setting sun. She was adamant that the children return from wherever they were playing before sunset. Tonight they were on a very short expedition to the park and back—only a matter of a few blocks. Florence was glad that they lived on a corner lot and in a house with so many windows. She could easily see the children playing from the living room, dining room, and kitchen. The light traffic on the street made Florence feel secure. There were no blind spots.

Arthur and Bucket came in with Presto, brimming over with another story to tell.

"When we got up to the fence," Bucket said, "there was a man there with a huge Great Dane." She gestured with her hand showing how tall the dog was compared to Presto.

"So we warned him, Mom," Arthur added.

"He really thanked us, and then he helped us put up the sign. His dog's name was Tiny. Isn't that funny, Mom?" laughed Bucket.

"And he said he'd never, ever seen a coyote in the park!" Arthur said.

Chapter Twenty-Three

Gabriel and Gwyneth's Turn

LATER THAT NIGHT FLORENCE WENT INTO ARTHUR'S ROOM to tuck him in for the night. He wasn't there. Bucket wasn't in her room either. She headed downstairs thinking that they might be hiding on her. The basement was ideal, with its four rooms and unfinished laundry area. But it was empty too. Back upstairs the children surprised Florence by being in her own room. They were in their pajamas, sitting on her bed with the dog sprawled out beside them.

"Story time!" they both sang out.

Although the last three days had felt like an entire week to Florence, she rarely refused her children's story requests. She looked at the two of them and thought for a moment about the serendipity of their very existence. Although the marriage to Jean disintegrated, she was forever thankful that Arthur and Bucket were the result of that marriage. She couldn't imagine what life would have been like without them. She gratefully sat down with her children and began a new G and G story.

"It was spring. Gabriel and Gwyneth were home together on a Saturday. Their mother was attending a workshop for the day while the

kids were supposed to tidy their rooms and clean the kitchen. They had picked up their clothes and made their beds. Now they were in the kitchen making cookies. Flour smudges were on all the counter tops and the table. Bowls, measuring cups, and spoons were piled up high next to the sink. Two cookie sheets covered with oatmeal chocolate chip mounds of dough were lined up ready for their turn inside the oven. Gwyneth was wearing oven mitts, while Gabriel was bending down looking at his wrist watch.

"'Ten, nine, eight, seven, six, cing, quatre, tres, dos, uno! Out they come!'

"'Hurray for French and Spanish class!' she yelled as she retrieved the baked cookies.

"'Si, si, senorita,' said Gabriel as he deftly shovelled the cookies off of the sheets and onto the kitchen table. Gwyneth quickly put the next two lots of cookies into the oven.

"'Start timing Gabe,' she said. She turned around and looked at the mess. 'Oops. I guess we'd better start cleaning up.'" Gwyneth filled up the sink with hot, sudsy water. She made sure she had lots of suds. She looked over at Gabriel and then scooped up some foam from the sink and threw it at her brother. He caught the glob of whiteness on his cheek. He looked up, startled, and then smiled.

"'Muchos gracias Gwyn,' he said and pivoted around her to grab his own scoop of bubbles. He deposited this on the end of Gwyneth's nose as well as on the top of her head. It went back and forth between the two of them until there weren't very many suds left in the kitchen sink, but a great deal transferred to the floor and on each other's clothes.

"'What's that I smell,' Gwyneth shrieked. She snatched her oven mitts and skidded on the wet floor on the way to pull out the batch of cookies. Then she started laughing as she grabbed a cupboard handle just

in time to stop herself from falling to the floor.

"'Easy does it,' Gabriel cautioned, although he was laughing too. He hastily retrieved the cookies from the oven and placed them on the table.

"By this time Van Gogh had arrived, curious about all the commotion. He stopped at the doorway to the kitchen, not wanting to get his paws wet.

"'Look Gabe, it's Van Gogh...' Gwyneth bent down to talk to the cat.

"'Do you want a cookie?' Gabriel asked, picking one of the cookies and offering it to the cat.

"'Maybe the chocolate chips aren't good for him,' said Gwyneth. But the cat just sniffed, held his head high, and walked away, unimpressed."

◇ ◇ ◇

"Boy, cats aren't like dogs, are they," Arthur commented.

"That's for sure. Presto would have eaten that cookie in an instant!" Bucket agreed.

"Ahem," their mother said.

"OK, mom. But this is making me hungry," Arthur said with a twinkle in his eye.

◇ ◇ ◇

"It took quite a bit of time to clear up the kitchen. Gabriel did the floors first because they were so wet. Gwyneth carefully put the cooled cookies in the glass cookie jar that always sat on the counter right next to the stove. It was yellow with painted fruit on one side. Their mother had it when she was growing up. It held at least two dozen medium-sized cookies.

"Finally they were sitting down at the table in a neat and tidy room. The dishes were piled on the drying rack and on the counter beside it.

The last batch of cookies lay cooling underneath a tea towel. Gwyneth and Gabriel were each on their third cookie but showing signs of slowing down.

"'I think we should go outside, Gabe,' his sister suggested.

"'You're right. It's spring after all,' he agreed.

"'I wonder if Van Gogh would go for a walk with us? We have a leash for him, remember?'

"'I don't know. He doesn't like to get his paws messy,' Gabriel said and shook his head. 'I have an idea! Let's play hide-and-seek! Count to one hundred slowly. I'm going outside!' He dashed out to the back porch before Gwyneth could voice her objections.

"She started counting out loud. By the time she was at twenty, she had swept the crumbs off the table and pushed the chairs in. By forty she had captured Van Gogh and put him on his leash. At fifty she was out the door with her jacket on. By the number eighty, she had circled the house. She counted to one hundred at the top of her voice, standing in the back-yard looking out at the forest beyond, knowing full well Gabriel had headed out to the familiar network of pathways. Van Gogh was trying to get out of his collar and kept twisting his head back and forth. He was obviously not used to being controlled.

"'Coming, ready or not, Gabriel!' Gwyneth yelled at the top of her voice, giving her brother fair warning that she was on the hunt. Gwyneth opened the gate to their chain-link fence that surrounded the yard, encouraging the cat to pass through with her. She followed the pathway that led out into the thick of the trees. Because it was early spring, the leaves were just coming out on the branches, so she could see much further than if it had been the summertime.

"She walked to the place where they had found the bag of kittens,

wondering if Van Gogh would remember. He sniffed and gingerly walked around, mewing. Gwyneth bent down and patted him.

"'Don't worry, Van Gogh. You're safe with us now,' she said.

"There were some good hiding places among the clumps of bushes that grew between the taller trees. It was an aspen wood with lots of dips and little hills. There was a brook that wound its way through the forest as well. Gwyneth walked along its banks for a while, thinking Gabriel could hide himself under a low overhang of trees. She had to take her time because the cat liked to stop and sniff a branch or a rock. But there was still no sign of her brother.

"'Gabriel, Gabriel!' Gwyneth called out. She was hoping she might at least hear movement in the woods. Gabriel was known for changing his hiding place if he knew she was getting closer and if he could make a quick escape to somewhere further away.

"'I'm coming to get you, bro!' Gwyneth said and moved deeper into the forest. Van Gogh seemed more accustomed to the leash. She could walk quickly on the well-travelled pathways making sure to glance in the byways as she went. Sometimes she would stop and just listen for a footfall or a tell-tale sound of breaking twigs. There was nothing.

"Finally Gwyneth picked up Van Gogh and jumped across the stream several times to make sure she was not missing any little copse where Gabriel might hide. He was slender and so he was able to fold up into some pretty tiny spaces. After a while she was certain that she had investigated every possible forest niche.

"'Gabriel! Come out, come out wherever you are!' she yelled, putting down the cat. All she heard was the sound of a house finch and an early robin. Gwyneth looked up at the tall branches and turned round in a slow circle, looking for anything that might give her a hint of where Gabriel

might be. She couldn't even remember what jacket he was wearing. Now she was getting concerned.

"'Give me a hint, Gabe!' she cried out. Gwyneth turned around in another slow circle, this time in the opposite direction, hoping it would make a difference. Then she closed her eyes, put her hands over her face and really concentrated. She was trying to focus her listening and to think of where else Gabe could possibly be.

"When she finally opened her eyes, she saw something she really didn't want to see. It was Van Gogh's empty collar, with the leash hanging limply from her hand. How could the cat have escaped and Gwyneth not known it? Now she was in anguish. Van Gogh was gone and so was her brother!"

"Well I guess that's it, sport's fans," Florence said, grinning mischievously at Bucket and Arthur.

"Not again, mom!" Arthur objected.

"Yeah, you did that twice in a row. That's just not fair!" Bucket cried as she rubbed her eyes tiredly.

"What's not fair is if I don't take you to school on time tomorrow. The holiday doesn't start until the day after," their mother said. She ushered them into their respective bedrooms. At Bucket's room she knelt down beside her bed.

"I didn't tell you how much I enjoyed seeing your rehearsal," she said.

"You saw the rehearsal?" Bucket asked, looking at her mother with searching eyes.

"Well, I saw some of it. You and the other girls seemed to be having lots of fun up there." Her mother smiled.

"Yeah, it's fun. But I want to memorize the rest of my lines over the holidays. Will you help me mom?" Bucket asked.

"I look forward to it," her mother said, and leaned over to kiss her good night.

In Arthur's room, Florence noticed some eye patches on his bedside table. Arthur was already asleep. She smoothed his hair back and kissed his cheek. As she did so, she noticed that one of the pirate eye patches was ripped. She picked it up and took it out of the room. In the light of the hallway, it looked like it would need more than a few stitches to fix. Florence went to the basement for her sewing basket. She would mend it for Arthur tonight. Her son had taken a new interest in school since pirates had been introduced in Miss Mitchell's art class. He and Lance had made quite a few eye patches on the week-end. Maybe this was one that they needed in order to run their new pirate club. Florence smiled as she got out the black thread and needle. She'd ask Arthur about it in the morning.

Chapter Twenty-Four

Bad News/Good News

IT WAS THE LAST DAY OF THE SPRING TERM. Florence and the rest of the fine arts staff were assembled for some Easter treats in the staff room. Everyone was relaxed and talking about their holiday plans. A few were looking at their watches, mentally getting ready to leave. Carole Temple had joined them on the couches surrounding a low, wide coffee table. Elaine Savage entered the room. Florence could tell at a glance that she was not her usual up-beat self.

"Oh, I'm so glad you're all here," she started. The chatter stopped, and everyone turned to face her. She sat down heavily in a vacant arm chair.

"Is everything all right?" Carole asked.

"Well, actually it isn't. You know I've just come from the supervisor's meeting. There are always plenty of rumours to go around, but this has more than one source." She took a big breath and continued. "It looks like the Fine Arts Centre as we know it will be gone next year."

There was complete silence for a moment and then everyone started talking at once. Elaine held her hand up for quiet.

"I know how upsetting this must be, but I thought it would be better for you to hear the whole story from me rather than half-true rumours this holiday," she said in a weary voice.

"Will everyone lose their jobs?" Florence asked.

"I'm not sure," responded Elaine. "I can only say that the Fine Arts Centre will no longer exist. The whole funding structure has changed, so the powers that be are carving up the pie the way they want to. And we won't be getting a slice."

"But what about the fine arts in the school district?" Carole asked. "What are they going to do about that?"

"I have no idea. They have assured me that the supervisor position will not be touched, but beyond that they are not saying. Staffing begins after Easter, so they will have to get their plans together by then." Talk began immediately. Elaine let it go on for a while.

"Look, team," she said, bringing them back to silence. "The Fine Arts Centre had a good go. We've been lucky to keep it afloat for so long. And you have individually and collectively contributed so much to the arts. I can't tell you how lucky I've been to work with each and every one of you," she said, tearing up. Pretty soon everyone was crying, laughing, and getting up and hugging each other.

"I don't know what I'll do without the Centre," Carole said with a sigh.

"You are so talented, Carole, and such a good manager: you'll have no trouble getting a job. And that goes for all of you," Elaine said, addressing the whole group. "Make sure you take the opportunity after Easter to get your name out there. You are tremendous teachers and any principal would be happy to have you. I know I have been," she added with a trembling smile. This set off another wave of crying among all of the staff. Over the din a phone rang.

Carole stumbled over to her desk to retrieve it.

"It's for you Florence," she called. "She says her name is Miss Mitchell." As Florence moved to the back of the room behind the book cases, where she could take the call in privacy, everyone continued to sob and talk with each other. There was still a sense of disbelief.

"Hello Ms. Dunne," Miss Mitchell said. "How are you today?"

"Actually not that great—but that's another story. How can I help you? Is Arthur all right?" she asked, wondering why she was getting this phone call with the spring break almost upon them.

"Oh yes, Arthur is fine. It's just that I think I might know who has been tormenting him," Miss Mitchell explained.

"Well that is great news. I'm wondering how you figured it out?" quizzed Florence.

"Well, I got a shock this morning when I went into the art room to pick up the Jolly Rogers. I was going to iron them over the holidays."

"Arthur showed them to me when I went to the school on Wednesday night. I thought they looked amazing! Your class did a great job."

"Not anymore," Miss Mitchell said, sounding dejected. "Yellow paint was smeared over quite a few of the flags. In fact all of the flags have been damaged except one."

"I'm guessing that's how you knew the culprit," Florence observed. "His was the one that wasn't touched."

"Exactly," she agreed. "But there was another clue."

"Good. I am so relieved to know you've figured it out." Florence said.

"I am too Ms. Dunne," Miss Mitchell said. "It's been eating at me, and I wish I had tackled the issue sooner."

"But, now you've unravelled the problem," Florence assured her. "What was the second clue?"

"Well, the biggest clue was the yellow paint on a certain person's running shoe."

"What happened when you confronted this certain person with the evidence?"

"I'm afraid it was deny, deny, deny," admitted Miss Mitchell.

"Oh dear, then we can't really move forward. I was hoping to call and chat to the parents about the situation," said Florence.

"Don't worry, Ms. Dunne. Another person came forward and whispered in my ear. And this certain someone had yellow paint under his fingernails," Miss Mitchell said. "I was able to talk to both individuals at lunch recess today, which they missed. They had a lot of cleaning up to do."

"I'm sure Mr. Gizo was happy to help," Florence said.

"He certainly was," Miss Mitchell agreed. "My next calls are to the two sets of parents involved. I hope this will be the end of it."

"I hope so too," Florence sighed. "I would appreciate it if you'd give me the names of those two individuals. I have a feeling that they may be Arthur's bullies."

"I put their names in a sealed envelope in Arthur's back pack. I told him it was a notice about the costumes for *Pirates.* That's in there too, by the way. Looks like you're going to have a busy holiday," Miss Mitchell said.

"It's good to be busy. And thanks for your detective work. You don't know how much I appreciate this," said Florence with evident relief.

"You're welcome, Ms Dunne. I know I still have my work cut out for me in the last two months of school!"

"Enjoy your break, Miss Mitchell. You deserve it."

"I'm sure you do too. Good-bye for now." Florence hung up and put her head down. There were just too many things whirling around in her head. She didn't hear the footsteps that came softly up beside her. She felt a hand on her shoulder and looked up quickly.

"I hope it's not bad news," Elaine said, looking concerned. Florence realized that it didn't sound like anyone else was around. I wasn't surprising that the staff had left shortly after the shocking announcement. Elaine looked absolutely drained.

"Well actually it's good news of a sort, Elaine,' she said. "It's to do with some bullying incidents at Arthur's school. At least now I'll have time to deal with it." Florence stood up and gave Elaine a hug. "And I'm so sorry about the Centre!"

"I know you were promised this job back after the sabbatical. I'm really sorry too," said Elaine sadly. "It puts you out in limbo, doesn't it?"

"It's not an unfamiliar feeling," Florence said ruefully. "I have yet to be admitted to any university! I know I could enrol in three random courses here, but I did so want to start a master's program."

"You know you can use me for a reference anytime, Flo!" she said firmly.

"Thanks so much. What are you going to do about the fine arts in the schools, now that the Centre will be closing?" Florence asked with concern.

As the two women gathered up their things and moved slowly out of the staff room, they discussed the options that could be available to the school board. Elaine, although devastated, had seen the writing on the wall for quite some time. She was eager that all the members of the Fine Arts Team (They once got T-shirts with "FAT" written in bold letters.) find good placements in the school system. She had always said that the Centre was not a permanent fixture, that it was a government-granted project that only survived from application to application. But it meant a huge adjustment for a great many people, not the least of which was all the students who had enjoyed fine arts excursions in the past.

Both Florence and Elaine were happy that they had two more months left to enjoy the comings and goings at the Centre. They had already planned a night of celebration at one of the Moorland hotels. The evening would obviously take on a more poignant tone. Teachers from all grade levels and subjects in the fine arts annually came together to sing, laugh, eat, talk, and display their own art-work. It was a grand evening that was organized by the Centre staff and looked forward to by all the district teachers. It meant a great deal of work, but the Centre teachers were not averse to extra hours when they knew that their colleagues did the same at their own schools. Florence wondered who would organize it the following year.

Chapter Twenty-Five

Fox Valley Walk

THE NEXT DAY DAWNED WINDY AND COOL. Clouds scuttled across the sky. Florence was taking Presto for a walk out at the Clayton's' in the afternoon, the children having gone with their father the night before. They would not be back until Easter Monday. Because Edie wasn't coming, Florence and Jean had changed their holiday plans. Florence was actually thinking this would turn out to be a good thing, as it would give her time to work on the application to Tirovica, Anna Saxton's University.

The roads were clear and dry out to the acreage, but the wind buffeted her compact car. She was glad that she was wearing two layers. It might not be too windy in Moorland, but in the clear sweep of land around the Clayton's' place, it was guaranteed to be windier. Presto was still standing up in the back seat. Without Bucket and Arthur to encourage her to sit down, she got jostled with every bump and turn.

Dorothy was at the door waving from behind the glass and Whiskey was jumping up and down in front of her. Florence waved at them as she got Presto out of the car. Dorothy and Whiskey came out the door and down the front steps to greet them, laughing at the wind that blew their hair this way and that. Presto barked a friendly greeting.

"Good to see you, Flo," Dorothy said. "Jan's finishing up a painting and can't leave it. You know what watercolours are like!" Florence's ex-husband, Jean, had been a painter before he started his woodworking business.

"Yes I do," Florence said, having once participated in one of Jan's workshops.

"What's this I hear about the Centre closing?" Dorothy asked as they took the dogs down the ditch beside Fox Valley Road.

"I'm afraid it's really going to close," Florence admitted. "It's pretty devastating for everyone concerned. Elaine is being philosophical—I guess she has to be. She's got to continue next year with whatever remnants there are of the team—that's if there's anyone at all!"

"It's been a big part of the school system for a long time. I know Jan thrived there," added Dorothy.

"And everyone thrived when Jan was there!" Florence exclaimed. "I think she was the best art teacher! Plus her philosophy of teaching influenced everyone."

"Jan loved it there too. She got a chance to really enjoy herself as a teacher," Dorothy said. "But now that she's retired, all she wants to do is paint. She loves every minute of her freedom. And so do I!"

"I can hardly wait for her next art show," Florence said with enthusiasm. "Is that what she's working on now?"

"I don't think Jan would see it that way. She's just painting each day and doesn't plan on displaying her work, ever. It always comes as a surprise to her that anyone would be interested in buying the stuff!" Dorothy laughed.

"I think it's that attitude that inspired everyone at work. She didn't mind taking a risk to really challenge the kids. Everyone picked up on that spirit of adventure," Florence said, watching the way Presto and Whiskey ran ahead of them. Presto would circle back to the two women and then catch up with Whiskey.

"What will happen to you, Flo?" Dorothy asked.

"There will be no job at the Centre—that's for sure. They still have to guarantee me some kind of a job after my sabbatical, but what that will be at this point, I certainly don't know," Florence said with a shrug.

"At least you must have some idea what you'll be doing in September?"

"Actually, because I didn't get accepted for the master's here in Moorland, I'm applying out of province," Florence said, as they turned back for the homeward trek.

"Wow! That would be a big change,."

"I feel incredibly stupid that I didn't apply to several different universities in the first place. But I honestly didn't think that there would be a problem getting into Moorland."

"I guess you just thought that it would be easier too, with the children here in school. You're so settled in that lovely house you bought," Dorothy said soothingly.

"Help! Don't remind me!" Florence cried. Presto turned and looked at her with canine concern. Florence laughed and waved her on.

"It can't be an easy decision," Dorothy said as they climbed up the stairs to the front door of the Clayton's home.

"What's this about a decision?" Jan asked as she opened the

door to all of them. The dogs gladly lapped up the water that Jan had set out for them in two separate bowls.

"It's a very difficult decision—moving out of province to go to school next year," Florence explained.

"It certainly is!" Jan agreed. "If you don't mind my asking, how is Jean about the possibility of Bucket and Arthur being away for a whole year?"

"That's one of the big issues. When I talked with him, he agreed. His decision could have something to do with his new baby and the business venture he started. It will actually simplify life for him and Marie," Florence said, as she gratefully sat down for a hot cup of coffee with the two sisters.

"And it makes the year possible for you, Flo," Jan said encouragingly.

"What about the children?" Dorothy asked. "Do they have any idea that you're thinking of moving away for the year?"

"Actually they don't have any idea. They just know I have a year of study, and so far they assume it's here. I don't want to say anything until I know for sure. I have been in touch with Anna Saxton, and she's been very encouraging. But I have to jump through the hoops just like everybody else."

"You go for it, Flo," Dorothy said Jan nodded her head in agreement.

"We'll miss you and the kids—that's for sure," Jan said.

"Hey, I'm not gone for good yet!" Florence exclaimed. She got up and put their coffee cups in the sink. "You two have to put up with me for a little while longer."

As Florence drove away with Presto in the back seat, she reflected on how lucky she and the kids were to have such good friends. And the dog was lucky too. Whiskey was a great companion, always up for adventure. In fact Presto was tuckered out from the walk and was lying down on her blanket.

For the next few days Florence carefully filled out the Tirovica university application for graduate studies. In addition to all the forms, there was a comprehensive five-hundred-word essay on what she hoped to bring to the drama-in-education program that was a part of the drama department. Florence wryly thought that it was like a test run for her sabbatical year. She was used to doing reports for the Centre, but this piece of writing was much more personal. She did a few drafts before she felt she was articulating her philosophy of education clearly and succinctly. She mailed it to the university by priority post and only then did she allow herself some breathing space.

Chapter Twenty-Six

Last Day of Spring Break

THE WEEK OF SPRING BREAK FLEW BY. After Jean brought the children back, they were outside every day. Everyone got exercise, especially the dog. Presto was enjoying her unaccustomed daily walks in the park or out in the country. One day Florence took Arthur and Bucket to the Moorland Museum, which was a treasure trove of not just local history but also international art. There happened to be a showing called "Animals in Art." The exhibition spanned different media and included artists from around the world. They were transfixed by a Robert Bateman original painting of a mountain wolf.

"It reminds me of the coyote we saw," Arthur said.

"Yeah, but way more powerful. He looks bigger, don't you think, mom?" Bucket wondered aloud.

"Oh yes, he's much larger," agreed their mother. "Remember the wolves we heard when we were cross-country skiing near the mountains last year?"

"It was spooky!" Arthur said. "It sounded so lonely."

"Hey, guys," Bucket said, motioning them to come into the adjoining gallery. "There's a giant cow over here!" Sure enough, the large bovine was one of Joe Fafard's sculptures. It was done in cut metal pieces with a painted surface texture, giving it a curious three-dimensional effect. There were six others similar to it in the room.

"Come and stand in the middle!" called Arthur. Bucket and Florence joined him in the midst of the cows.

"See," Arthur said "It's just like being a part of the herd." They all laughed. Their mother started mooing followed both by Arthur and Bucket. Soon enough the gallery guard came over.

"Please let other people enjoy the exhibit too," he said, but not in an unfriendly way.

"I'm so sorry," Florence apologized. "We got carried away." She shepherded the children to the mezzanine of the museum.

"Mom! You're a bad influence on us," Bucket said, with her hands on her hips.

"You have to miss recess," reprimanded Arthur.

"You're tough customers, you know that?" Their mother laughed. "Since this is the last night before you go back to school, how about we go out for pizza?"

"Yes, let's!" they both agreed. As they drove away from downtown Moorland to the suburbs, Florence thought that the exhibit had been very rewarding. As if reading her thoughts, Bucket said,

"There are so many beautiful animals in the world. Maybe it would be fun to be a vet at the zoo."

"Oh yeah, Bucket. That would be fun," Arthur said. "But I'd be a little nervous around the lions and tigers."

"Don't be silly, Arthur. They get tranquilized before you treat them," Bucket said with authority.

Florence wondered if Bucket's dream of being a veterinarian

would be realized. She was only ten, soon to be eleven. It was good to have something to wish for. All too often life had a way of interfering with even a carefully laid plan. At least, that was Florence's experience. She hoped that Bucket had enough determination to bring her dream into reality. Florence would certainly do everything she could to help her achieve it, if that's what she wanted.

That evening, after the children were asleep, Florence sat in the living room contemplating the phone numbers of the two children from Arthur's class who had defaced the pirate flags. The culprits were Henry and Greg. She had already talked to Henry's mother the first week-end of the spring break. Her reaction was disbelief that anything untoward could be happening at school. Florence later got a return call from Henry's mother, sheepishly admitting that Henry was taking part in harassment activities. Then she said that, according to her son, the leader behind the various schemes was Greg. Miss Mitchell's suspicions were confirmed: the children who tried to destroy the Jolly Rogers were the same ones who were bullying Arthur.

Florence was somewhat apprehensive about getting in touch with Greg's parents. She had thought about the situation for the entire spring break and finally came up with a possible solution. She would ask Arthur's father to make the phone call. Florence reasoned that a call from Mr. Boisvert would have more of an impact. So she picked up the phone and called her ex-husband. After inquiries about the health of each other's children, Florence broached the subject.

"I wanted to discuss the bullying Arthur's been getting at school. You know that I talked to Henry's mother."

"Yes, and it sounded like she needs to keep a closer watch on her son. It's a good thing he admitted to everything else that's been going on with Arthur,."

"That was the breakthrough all right," Florence agreed. She took a deep breath and said, "I'd like you to get in touch with Greg's parents tonight, if you have the time," she asked. Her ex-husband had been so busy in the last few years that Florence had gotten used to being a single parent in every sense of the word. But she felt that this situation was too important for her to go it alone.

"Can do. What's your thinking?" he asked.

"I don't think Greg's admitted to anything. It was Henry who told Miss Mitchell in the first place about what they did to the pirate flags. Now he's coming clean about other things he and Greg were doing. But Greg has not said he has done anything wrong."

"I get it. I can't assume anything when I talk to them," Jean responded.

"That's right. I'll give you their number." A moment later she heard a baby crying in the background.

"Sorry, got to go," Jean said and rang off.

Florence was relieved but still worried that Jean would not have time tonight to phone Greg's parents. She thought that it was extremely important that these people knew before school began again. She sighed and muttered to herself, "Damn! Maybe I should have made the call." But the dye was cast. She prayed that at least Henry's attitude would be different tomorrow. Maybe that would have an effect on Greg, even if Jean didn't make the call.

Florence got up and went into Bucket's room. She saw the script to *Pirates of Penzance* on her bedside table. With a little help from

Arthur, she had gotten almost the whole libretto memorized. Right now she was stuck on the "duty" speech in act two. It was the kind of monologue that had to be understood clearly first. Bucket was working through it slowly before trying to memorize it. So much of Gilbert and Sullivan was a play on words. Florence admired Mrs. Cauldwell for taking on the musical. She thought that it was a stretch for grades five and six, but in a good way. Florence reasoned that because it was such a challenge, the cast would probably never forget the experience.

When she went into Arthur's room, she petted Presto, who was nestled beside him on the bed. Arthur lay curled up in a fetal position with the dog at his back. His sketch book lay under his hand. She bent down and gently eased it out, putting the covers up over his shoulder as she straightened up. Florence tip-toed out of the room and closed the door softly.

In the confines of her room, Florence sat down with the book in her hands. She hadn't looked at it since she read the poem about rain. She had a battle with herself about whether or not she should be invading her son's privacy. But worries about his psychological state after dealing with the schoolyard bullies won out. There were a lot of sketches Arthur had done, even some of his new baby sister. But there was a page of doodles and words hidden in the images:

The dog licks my hand
She is always happy to see me
Wolf is cousin to the dog
I know the wolf would bite my hand
Being a vet could be dangerous

Florence wondered about Arthur's thought processes in this poem. He seemed to be recognizing the difference between domestic and wild. Perhaps he was also coming to terms with that in the schoolyard. There were kids he could trust and others that he definitely could not. In that respect it was quite a profound piece of writing.

She closed the book thoughtfully, held it close, and tiptoed back to Arthur's room. Placing it on his bedside table, she looked at him with fresh eyes. His was a sensitive soul. Florence hoped he always would be and that life would not take that away from him. She also hoped that the bullying Arthur had experienced would not haunt him in the future. Now that the perpetrators were found, Arthur and his friends should be able to enjoy the rest of the school year.

Chapter Twenty-Seven

Just a Bunch of Nonsense

At choir practice that week, Lance and Arthur were sitting at the back of the rehearsal room having a snack and talking.

"I got to go snorkelling," Lance said, telling Arthur about his trip to Mexico. "There were these cool fish, all different colours. And the water was so warm!"

"Amazing," Arthur responded.

"My mom went parasailing, but my dad said I was too little. Maybe next year," he said with confidence.

"Parasailing would be the best. I'd like to do that," Arthur said wistfully.

"What'd you do?"

"We walked the dog a lot. I biked everywhere." Arthur was searching for something that sounded interesting. "We went to this museum and saw lots of animals, even a giant cow."

"A giant cow?"

"Yeah, there was a whole herd of them," explained Arthur. "Hey, do you still have your eye patch?" he asked.

"Course. I took it to Cabo. Dad was mad 'cause I kept wearing it." Lance laughed. "I'll bring it tomorrow, OK?"

"Sure. Seymour told me he's got his. Add's gonna bring his too," Arthur said with a smile.

"Argh!" growled Lance.

In the girl's washroom, Providence and Rowena were combing their hair and talking to Bucket. They were huddled around the two mirrors.

"I can't believe you've almost got all your lines memorized, Bucket," exclaimed Rowena. "My song is so hard. My mom made me listen to it every day of the holidays and I still haven't got it!"

"Practice, practice, practice," sang Providence. The girls looked at her, annoyed. "Hey, don't give me those dirty looks. That's what Mrs. Cauldwell says all the time!" Bucket and Rowena started to playfully punch Providence, who then ran out of the washroom.

"Help me! Help me!" she yelled, half laughing. "I'm being attacked by murderous demons." Bucket and Rowena were fast on her heels and had just started to chase her around the big rehearsal room when Mrs. Black clapped eyes on them.

"Girls, really! Save your energy for rehearsal!" she yelled. They skidded to a halt, laughing.

"We're going to begin in a minute anyway, *ladies*," Ms. Moster added. She had just entered the room with Carey Biggs. Carey sat down at the piano and began playing while Ms. Moster walked to her music stand. As soon as the opening chords rang out, children started to filter back to the rehearsal room. Carey began by playing a lively polka but soon moved into his own rendition of popular music tunes. Pretty soon children were gathering around the piano singing along. After a few minutes, when everyone seemed to be assembled, Carey stopped playing the piano and shooed them back to their seats.

Ms. Moster held up her hands for quiet.

"I have one very big announcement to make." She paused to let her words sink in. "I'm afraid this will be the last concert for Mr. Biggs." There was an immediate chorus of objection. All eyes were on Carey.

"I've accepted a position at the University of Moorland, teaching students piano. As you can probably guess, most of my teaching will be after school, so I can't continue with the children's choir," he said. "But I may come on tour with you next year. It's a big *if*. Who knows?" At that hopeful promise, the choir clapped.

"We have certainly enjoyed the last three years you have been with us Mr. Biggs," Ms. Moster stated.

"I'm not gone yet!" Mr. Biggs said cheerily.

"I certainly hope not! We still have a lot of work to do!" Mrs. Black walked in the door and waved to Ms. Moster.

"Oh yes, Mrs. Black just reminded me," Ms. Moster said. "Please don't forget about the tour forms. We need those in by the June performance. I know that may seem like weeks away, but that will be here before you know it. Your parents really need the time to plan. We'll send another notice home when it gets closer to the due date. Are there any questions?"

"Could you cancel if you, like, couldn't raise enough money in time?" Providence asked, with real concern.

"Don't worry about that, Pro," Mrs. Black said soothingly. "Your parents will be given all the information they need. And you know they can always call me if they have any questions. They can call me right now if they want to."

"And now let's get back to singing, choristers!" Ms. Moster reminded them. "Have a look at the Jenkins piece, please. Who remembers anything about this composer?"

"I do!" Lance yelled, as he waved his hand in the air enthusiastically.

"OK, Lance, let's hear it," encouraged Ms. Moster.

"This piece is just a bunch of nonsense!" Lance said, causing everyone to laugh.

"What do you mean by that?" Ms. Moster asked, undeterred.

"Jenkins just wanted people to listen to the music, so he made up words that sounded good with the music," Lance explained.

"That reminds me of the third thing I needed to tell you," said Ms. Moster. "I would like you, the choristers, to introduce the songs for this concert. And Lance—you are the first one chosen. You can do the introduction for Jenkins' piece, 'Adiemus.'"

"Sure thing, Ms. Moster," responded Lance. He looked at Arthur and gave him the thumbs-up. Arthur responded in kind.

At the end of the rehearsal, most of the kids crowded around Mr. Biggs. Many were hugging him, to which he responded with, "But I'm not gone yet!" many times. It was difficult to get everyone to leave until Mrs. Black came downstairs. She admonished the children for leaving their parents waiting for them. Mrs. Black never spoke to the choristers sharply; she was just firm in a congenial way. Everyone knew that they had to listen to her, and soon the place cleared out.

Chapter Twenty-Eight

Places Everyone!

A REHEARSAL OF A VERY DIFFERENT KIND took place a few weeks later in the gym of Bannister Elementary School. The place was being set up for the first time with scenery and props. Mrs. Cauldwell had ushered the cast into three rows of chairs next to the piano. Ms. Moster was also there to help out with the first run-through of act one. She was doing vocal warm-ups with the children while Mrs. Cauldwell arranged the score on her music stand. Mr. Harbicht was on the stage at the far end of the gym talking to a few students who were standing with the "rocks" for the first act in their arms.

"Now children," Mr. Harbicht was saying, "remember that the sides are papier-mâché, so please be careful."

"Yes, Mr. Harbicht," the students said in unison.

"Please look on the underside of your rock. You will notice a large letter on the bottom printed in black felt. There is a matching letter taped to the stage. Please put your rock on that letter with the rough side facing out." One by one each student found their letter and placed the rock on the stage. Then they hopped off the stage and stood in the audience to admire their handiwork.

"You did an excellent job of making the rocks look realistic,"

Mr. Harbicht said. "The stage lights at the big theatre will be even stronger, so I don't think anyone made their set piece too dark. Good work everyone!"

"Yeah!" they cheered spontaneously. By this time the cast had carried their chairs over to the stage, remarking on the set design that they were seeing for the first time. Mrs. Cauldwell and Ms. Moster wheeled the piano over.

"You and your team did quite the job creating those rocks, Mr. Harbicht," Mrs. Cauldwell said appreciatively. "Can you stand on them? Will they take any weight?"

"Absolutely. The tops are solid. They're actually stools that have been faced with paper, gauze, glue, and paint," Mr. Harbicht explained. "On the other side we painted the stone ruins for act two."

"That's ingenious!" Ms. Moster exclaimed, just as Arthur walked in with most of the pirate flags. Because Arthur always stayed for Bucket's rehearsals, the teachers often put him to work. He was happy to help out with the pirate flags since his class was the one to create them. Jan Clayton had been able to wash off the offending paint streaks simply using water. Although the paint for the flags was acrylic, Greg and Harvey had used tempera block paint. A faint bit of yellow paint could be seen where it had gotten on the black cloth. Miss Mitchell had spent some time gently sponging that out too before she ironed each one. Once waving on the poles, no-one would be able to tell otherwise.

"My favourite's the sea. It looks real," Arthur said, carrying the Jolly Roger flags that were now attached to bamboo poles. Everyone looked at the backdrop that Mr. Harbicht's art team had constructed.

"It took two weekends just to make the flats," explained Mr. Harbicht. "I had a group of dedicated parents to help me. Jan Clayton sketched out the design for the seashore and showed the students how to do the painting for it."

"This is such a big undertaking," Mrs. Cauldwell stated, "that a simple thank-you seems hardly adequate."

"Don't thank me yet. We've got a long way to go before the act two backdrop is ready," he cautioned.

"That's quite all right," Mrs. Cauldwell remarked. "We aren't ready for it anyway!"

"Please stay for the rehearsal if you want, Mr. Harbicht," Ms. Moster offered.

"Thanks, but I don't want to spoil the surprise," he said, smiling. "All right, my group, let's get back to the art room and clean up." Off they went, some of the students waving to those in the cast they knew as they left. Mrs. Cauldwell turned to the seated students.

"The whole cast is here today for act one because I think it's important that everyone be aware of what's happening in the entire musical. That's why you're present, policeman's group. Even though you don't come on stage until act two, I want you to see this part of the show. You can give important feedback to the cast as well. Ms. Moster will now tell you how this rehearsal will run."

"Pirates, you'll line up in order against the gym wall. Arthur will give you your flags that you're going to wave as you enter during the overture," said Ms. Moster indicating where they should stand. "Girl's chorus and the major general, sit in the back two rows in your order to come on stage. Policemen, you are at ease in the first two rows!"

Providence, Bucket, and then Rowena were the last three in the last row of the Girl's Chorus. Providence leaned over Bucket to whisper to Rowena.

"I love your costume, Major General."

"Me too. They haven't got the hat ready yet. I can hardly wait."

"I'll be wearing one of Pro's dresses," Bucket said in hushed tones. "It's really pretty too, but I haven't tried it on yet."

"It was one of my two favourite dresses," Providence said. "And I'm wearing my other favourite."

"Girls," Mrs. Cauldwell cautioned, "you must show good audience manners throughout the rehearsal, starting now!"

"Yes, Mrs. Cauldwell," the girls sang out in unison, looked at each other with raised eyebrows, and didn't say another word.

Chapter Twenty-Nine

News

THAT FRIDAY, FLORENCE AND THE CHILDREN arrived home to find quite a few letters and magazines inside the mail slot of their front door. Bucket and Arthur were distracted by Presto's enthusiastic welcome, while Florence quickly spotted a brown envelope from the University of Tirovica. She placed it under the *Owl* magazine and all of the bills that seemed to collect at the end of the month. And then she noticed it—a card with children's printing on it addressed to Arthur.

"Arthur," his mother said. "Here's a card in the mail for you." Arthur and Bucket were playing catch with Presto in the living room. Presto loved to play with the children's stuffed animals, especially the white ones. Florence was frequently tossing them in the wash to keep the stains at bay.

"A card for me?" Arthur questioned.

"Well, it has your name on it! Come and see," his mother said, holding out the card.

"I wonder who it could be?" Bucket asked, coming over to watch Arthur open the envelope. Sometimes they got mail from their grandfather and their cousins, but it wasn't even a monthly occurrence.

"It's a birthday party invite," Arthur said looking at the front of the card. His joy turned to puzzlement when he opened it up. "It's from Henry."

"Yes, it is," his mother confirmed, leaning over and reading the card. "It's lucky we got it today. The party's on Sunday!"

"You don't look that excited," Bucket noticed. "I've never really heard you talk about him. It's always 'Add this,' or 'Lance that.' Sometimes you talk about Seymour and Lau, but never Henry."

"I don't have to go, do I, mom?" Arthur asked imploringly.

"We can talk about it. We've got time," Florence assured him. Usually when she used the "we'll talk about it" line, it meant that Bucket or Arthur would wind up doing what she suggested. There was always a lot of talk going on in their household.

As the children were getting ready for bed that night, Florence stole into her bedroom and retrieved the brown envelope. With shaky hands she pulled out an official-looking document. It was her acceptance letter into graduate studies at the drama department at the University of Tirovica! She couldn't believe her good fortune. Her father had retired to Tirovica when Arthur was a toddler, so it would be an opportunity for her children to connect with a grandparent whom they really didn't know.

Her hands were still unsteady as she looked at the rest of the documentation. When Florence saw the fee schedule on the last page, she sat down on her bed, and read and re-read the columns of numbers. A sabbatical year was wonderful in many respects, but it meant a 40 per-cent reduction of income. She had also been advised that she should set a certain amount aside so she could buy back her teaching year for pensionable service. The other big commitment was a monthly debit for the children's education fund. She was absolute about continuing to finance this. Dorothy Clayton had strongly advised her not to forego the payments. Arthur and Bucket had certificates hanging on their bedroom walls that showed they were enrolled in a scholarship program. She had only been tithing to the organization for the last two years, but she knew that her children would need the help, and she was determined that their opportunities should never be limited.

Florence shook her head, realizing she must have been naïve about the financial impact the sabbatical would have on her family. Not only did the University of Tirovica require an initial instalment by the end of August; there were also steep maintenance fees following her year of studies. This fee schedule continued until her thesis was completed. She guessed this was motivation to get your degree as soon as possible. Florence was just starting to panic as figures flew through her mind when Presto came bounding into the room with yet another stuffy. She forced the papers back into the envelope and placed it upside down on the bed.

"You crazy dog!" she said and bent over, trying to get the fuzzy bear out of the dog's mouth. Presto liked to tease and would play tug-of-war with her. Then Florence would pretend to move away, wait a moment, and lunge to grab the toy. Quite often this strategy worked. This time it didn't, so Florence had to play the game again. And again. Bucket appeared at her doorway.

"Gee, Mom," Bucket laughed, "Presto's got your number."

"Come and help me out," her mother challenged. So Bucket crouched on one side, while Florence coaxed the dog on the other. But Presto only growled if they got anywhere near the stuffy. Finally

Arthur's curiosity got the better of him, and he looked in too.

"You guys are pathetic," he said. "Me 'n Presto are pals. I'll show you how it's done." So he went over to the dog, knelt down, and petted her back first, saying, "There girl. It's OK. You just wanna have fun, dontcha?" Then he stroked her head and with his free hand quietly eased out the fuzzy bear.

"That's amazing, Arthur," his sister said with real respect. "Maybe *you* should be the veterinarian."

"No way, it's all yours, Bucket. Presto's just a good dog, aren't ya?" Arthur gave the dog an affectionate squeeze.

"Mom! Can we hear the rest of the G and G story?" Bucket asked.

"Yeah," agreed Arthur. "We wanna know what happened."

"All right you two, *if* you can get into your pajamas in five minutes, with your teeth brushed!"

"Deal!" they both said at once and disappeared down the hallway to their bedrooms.

Florence returned to the brown envelope, picked it up, and thought what a change in all of their lives it would mean. She had fought hard to give her children a stable home life. She had recoiled at the thought of attaching herself to any man, even in a casual way. Florence had heard of women who reacted to divorce by having a string of affairs. She thought this might be a way of thumbing one's nose at the ex-husband, as if to say, "See how attractive I really am."

Florence had had the opposite reaction. She wanted to simplify her life, not complicate it. She just wanted to concentrate on what was important: her family and her work. Full stop. End of story. However, now that the children were older and so much more independent than when she was first divorced, she sometimes longed for the solace of adult companionship. But Florence would not want to bring just anyone into her family. He would have to be trustworthy, empathetic, and respectful of her two children. She abhorred the idea of a procession of overnight guests. And now here she was, wilfully yanking her family out of their safe harbour, launching out into unknown waters. When would she tell Bucket and Arthur?

Chapter Thirty

Van Gogh, The Mystery Cat

"We're ready Mom!" Bucket called. Florence put the envelope on her night stand and went to Bucket's room, where the kids and the dog were ready and waiting. She sat down heavily in the desk chair, kicked off her shoes, and put her feet up on the bed next to Presto. She gazed fondly at her two children.

"Van Gogh escaped," Arthur reminded Florence. His mother took no notice and sat back in the chair, closed her eyes and pretended to snore.

"Mom!" Bucket yelled. "You've got to tell us the rest of the story! Wake up!!"

"Alright, alright—if you're ready?" she teased.

"Yeah, we're ready!" Arthur said.

"Ready, ready, ready, ready, ready!" chimed in Bucket.

"Message received."

"Gwyneth couldn't believe how quickly the cat had disappeared. She picked up the leash and started calling for her, 'Van Gogh, Van Go-ogh!' She thought the cat, being so particular, would keep to the beaten pathway rather than venturing right through the undergrowth. But which way had the cat gone on the path—behind or ahead of where Gwyneth was standing?

"Trying to calm her racing heart, she crouched down, looking behind her. She didn't see anything other than trees and bushes. She crept forward on the trail, ever so carefully.

"Van Gogh had never been in the forest before and might be frightened. It was really important that the cat be caught as soon as possible. Suddenly she thought she saw the tip of Van Gogh's tail. Gwyneth figured she didn't have time for second-guessing and ran as fast as she could in pursuit.

"Around the next bend of the trail, she confirmed her original sighting. Van Gogh, though multi-coloured, had a completely white tail, which she held straight up in the air at all times. That white tail was like a flag for Gwyneth, beckoning her ever onward.

"It was hard to jog on the woodland pathways because of overhanging branches and some of the undergrowth that spread out in the spring. But Gwyneth was gaining on the cat after the next curve. She could almost see her floppy ear!

"Then Gwyneth realized with a start that Van Gogh was taking her close to the community dump. Gabriel had never hidden there before. This thought reminded Gwyneth that, in her excitement to catch the cat, she had almost forgotten about finding her brother. She started calling for her brother too.

"'Ga-briel! Ga-briel! Come back Van Gogh. Come here,' she yelled as loud as she could.

"Gwyneth could see the cat in plain sight now. She also noticed that the pathway was getting smaller. The woods thinned out abruptly, and they were at the far end of one of the mounds of refuse. This pile didn't stink because the community had different zones for each type of garbage. This particular one was for household effects.

"Gwyneth couldn't believe her eyes. Van Gogh was delicately stepping through the pile of trash: ripped couches, old two-legged chairs, rolls of mouldy carpet, washing machines, stacks of any shape or size of sinks, very stained toilets. It seemed like an endless assortment of someone's worst suburban nightmare. The cat was undeterred and kept on moving. Bucket was slowing down now, watching where she was walking.

"The cat appeared to stop. Gwyneth was so thankful. She was getting tired of looking for a safe pathway around all of the garbage. She bent down to pick up Van Gogh, but the cat just hopped away from her and gingerly walked further on. Gwyneth sighed and followed.

"'Come on, Van Gogh. Stop. We need to find Gabriel,' she pleaded. The cat turned and looked at her and meowed loudly as she jumped up onto an old white fridge.

"'Now I've got you, cat!' cried Gwyneth in triumph as she grabbed for her. But the cat eluded her still. This time she didn't move on. Van Gogh kept meowing and jumping up onto the refrigerator. Every time Gwyneth made a move to catch her, the cat would somehow escape her grasp.

"'You are impossible Van Gogh!' yelled Gwyneth in exasperation. She stood stock still for a moment, puffing heavily from trying to catch the cat. Suddenly the fridge moved. Gwyneth rubbed her eyes and looked again. This time when it moved, the cat jumped on it again, meowing loudly. An idea suddenly coalesced in Gwyneth's mind.

"Gabriel, is that you?' she asked, stepping close to the fridge, nose-to-nose with Van Gogh. In answer, the refrigerator moved again.

"Gabriel, you are crazy!' she screamed. Then she saw with horror that the handle to the door was broken. She tried to open the fridge grasping what she could but it remained stuck. Gwyneth tried again and again, but it wouldn't budge at all. The fridge kept moving in little bursts.

"'Gabe, don't move,' Gwyneth yelled. 'You're going to use up too much oxygen!' Then she noticed that the cat had moved off to the side and was meowing again.

"'What have you got this time, cat?' Gwyneth demanded as she moved to the cat's spot. And there, right beside Van Gogh, was a broken snow shovel with its handle missing. Gwyneth hopped over the junk back to the refrigerator with the shovel in hand.

"'Gabe, stay perfectly still. I have an idea.' Gwyneth took the corner of the shovel and tried to wedge it just underneath the defunct handle of the refrigerator door. It took a lot of strength to just position the edge of the shovel. Gwyneth pushed and pushed as hard as she could. It seemed to go in just an inch. Carefully Gwyneth levered the end of the shovel to pry the door open. Then the corner of the shovel snapped off and sent Gwyneth backward onto an old sofa. A rusted spring poked her in the side.

"'Ouch, you stupid sofa! Don't worry, Gabe,' she cried and stood up, 'I'll try again. I still have three more corners to go!'

"It was on the third corner, this time pushing as hard as she could that Gwyneth was able to get the shovel further in between the seals of the door. With great care and determination, she levered the door open. Gabriel came out with a whoosh, pushing hard on the door himself, gasping for air.

"'Sis, am I ever glad to see you,' he cried, giving her a fierce hug.

"'You don't have me to thank you know,' she said, a little bit teary.

"'What do you mean?' he asked..

"'Van Gogh brought me here. She is the one you should really thank!' Gwyneth admitted.

"'But I thought you weren't going to bring her,' Gabriel said.

"'I decided the cat needed to get used to the collar. And Van Gogh's

never been in the forest,' she explained. Gabriel looked around to thank his liberator.

"'You're making that up Gwyn. I don't see any cat here at all!' said Gabriel. And sure enough, there was no sign of Van Gogh.

"But I have the leash,' Gwyneth said in triumph.

"'And where is that?' Gabriel asked. Gwyneth looked all around the refrigerator, but it wasn't to be found.

"'I'm telling you the truth Gabe,' she said, now truly befuddled. "I know I'll find it somewhere. I must have dropped it while I was prying the door off the fridge. You've got to believe me!"

"'Listen, sis, I am just so happy you found me—I don't care how you did it!' So the two siblings walked arm in arm back to their home. As they rounded the corner, they saw Van Gogh, sitting in her favourite spot on a deck chair in the back-yard, calmly cleaning her front paws.

"'Come on, Van Gogh, tell Gabe the truth,' Gwyneth chided the cat as they sat down beside her. The cat meowed and continued her cleaning ritual.

"'You have to admit one thing, sis,' Gabriel said.

"'And what's that?' she asked.

"'It was one heck of a hiding place!' Gabriel said triumphantly. Gwyneth got up and started to tickle him unmercifully."

Chapter Thirty-One

Sisters

"THAT WAS A CRAZY STORY, MOM," Arthur said. "It would have been awful stuck in that refrigerator." He shivered.

"The best part was at the end," Bucket grinned. "When Gwyneth tickled her brother unmercifully!" Bucket started to tickle Arthur. He laughed helplessly. Then their mother joined in the fray. Presto jumped off the bed and started barking. They barely heard the phone ring above the noise they were making.

"I'll get it!" Bucket cried and launched herself through the doorway.

"All right Arthur, bedtime for you." His mother drew back the covers and he crawled in. "I agree that it would be terrible to be cooped up like that."

"Yeah, it was pretty lucky he was found," Arthur said.

"He was very lucky. Sometimes something that starts out bad can end up being good, don't you think?" his mother asked.

"I guess so," Arthur responded.

"I know so, Arthur James. Have a good night's sleep and I'll see you in the morning." Florence pulled up the blankets around him and kissed him on the cheek.

"I love you mom," murmured Arthur.

"And I love you two, three and four," whispered his mother. She stood up and turned out the lights as she left the room. She met Bucket coming down the hallway.

"It's for you mom. It's Aunt Edie."

"Thanks, dear. Arthur's almost asleep. Maybe you should go to bed too." She kissed Bucket and gave her a hug. "I'll come in when I'm off the phone."

"Hello, Edie. I guess you had a bit of a chat with my daughter," Florence began.

"That girl is growing up too fast," Edie said. "I can't believe how quickly the time's going. I really missed seeing the kids at Easter."

"We missed you and Wilt too. It was pretty quiet, but then that was OK considering what's going to happen." Florence quietly shut the door to the hallway that led to the bedrooms.

"Like the calm before the storm?" Edie questioned. "What storm are you talking about, Flo?"

"I just got my acceptance to the University of Tirovica," Florence admitted.

"Oh, Florence, that's absolutely amazing!" screamed Edie into the phone. "I am so happy for you."

"Thanks so much, sis. I didn't really know what to expect, so it came as a big surprise."

"This is just the best thing that ever happened to you in a long, long time, Flo."

"To tell you the truth, I'm a little numb. I spent some time looking at the fee schedule. The financial end of it is quite daunting," Florence said sombrely.

"Look, Flo, it's only for a year. Just bite the bullet," Edie said with steely determination. "Five years from now, you won't even remember the pinch you were in." When Florence didn't respond, she added, "This is opportunity staring you in the face. You'd never forgive yourself if you let it slip through your fingers. There is no comparison between getting your masters and three pick-up classes at your hometown U. And don't you go up a pay scale if you get this?" she demanded.

"OK, I know you're right Edie. I just started to think about what a leap this is. I'll have to rent this house, find a place in Tirovica, move, find a school that I can enrol the kids in..."

"Come on, Flo, you're not a wimp. Look at how you bought that house in the first place. That took a lot of guts to move and do everything you did!" Edie exclaimed, getting exasperated.

"When you put it that way, then I know I can do this. I'll just make a list of what I have to do and start hacking away at it."

"But this isn't just for you, Flo. Arthur and Bucket are at the perfect age for a change of pace. Their hormones haven't started kicking in, and they're young enough to be eager for something new. Tirovica is on an island. That island is a fascinating place with wildlife and some of the biggest trees in the world."

"I haven't told them yet," Florence said quietly.

"What?" Edie exclaimed, incredulous.

"Well I wanted to make sure that it was a done deal. I'm not sure how they'll react," Florence said with a sigh.

"They are going to be tickled pink. And if they aren't, they'll have three months to get used to the idea." Edie was always one to deal with obstacles as they occurred, and when they arose, she put a positive slant on overcoming them.

"And that's plenty of time for me to sort through everything too," Florence reasoned.

"Of course it is. And it's enough time for Wilt and I to make our travel plans to come and visit you. We've always wanted to tour the island; now this is reason enough," Edie said decisively.

"Let me see—I'll pencil you in for two weeks next July?" Florence teased.

"You do that sister!" Edie laughed.

"Thanks for your infusion of optimism Edie. It's been a long week."

"Anytime you need to talk, I'm here. Love you, Flo. Bye for now," Edie said, ringing off.

When Florence hung up, she went back to Bucket's room to say good night. Bucket was already fast asleep. Florence bent down to kiss her on the cheek, when she noticed the dog-eared script from the musical still in her hands. She removed it and put it on Bucket's bedside table. She gazed at her daughter, wondering if Bucket would be disappointed in not going on the children's choir tour next summer. She could probably not have afforded it, but with the impending move to the island, it would be completely out of the question. Surely there would be choirs where they were going? The more she thought about her daughter, the more she was convinced that with her outgoing nature she would have no trouble finding a niche in a new milieu.

Florence went over to Arthur's bedroom. He hadn't moved a muscle since she'd tucked him in. Presto was on the bed as usual, spread out on the bottom half. She raised her head when Florence came in the room and wagged her tail, thumping it on the bed.

Florence patted the dog and looked at her son. Her heart gave a leap when she thought of what he had been through this year. As far as she knew, there had been no new incidents, but Arthur was not the kind to broadcast his feelings or tell her of his problems the way her daughter always did. The move would not be as easy for him because he was a more reserved child. However, it might prove to be the best thing for him. He could break contact with the bullies on the playground. Florence wanted her children to feel they could handle their own problems and never to run away from difficulties. She knew instinctively that it was the right choice to get Arthur away from his tormentors. Florence fervently hoped that he would flourish once he was away from what had been causing him so much pain.

She was happy that Henry's parents were taking the situation in hand. She hadn't thought they would issue an invitation to the birthday party but was glad that they did. Since Arthur began in kindergarten, there had always been little cliques formed among the boys. Florence speculated that Henry was a bit of a follower and just needed some guidance. She knew that it was sometimes hard for a parent to distinguish between rough play and outright aggression. She wondered if Arthur would like to go to Henry's party. She'd have to phone Addison's and Lance's mothers to find out if their children were invited too. That would help!

Chapter Thirty-Two

The Words are All Nonsense

The rest of the month of May disappeared in a heat wave unusual for Moorland. People who had never considered having air-conditioning purchased one. The night of the final concert of the Moorland Children's Choir was uncommonly humid and hot, causing all the doors in the concert hall to be propped wide open. Luckily there were no busy roads nearby that would cause a noisy distraction.

Lance's mother had called Florence to say he had come down with a severe stomach ache right after school. Arthur was now going to introduce Jenkins' number. Florence was surprised at how calmly Arthur responded. He had come up with some words of introduction without that much help from her. He hadn't appeared worried about speaking in front of a crowd either.

Florence found a spot in the middle at the back of the auditorium. She noticed that people were using their programs for fans. The lights dimmed and only Carey Biggs came out on stage. He went directly to the piano, turned to the audience and smiled. Everyone hushed, and then he started to play.

Children came down the aisles of the auditorium, singing as they slowly walked toward the stage. Ms. Moster led one group while Mrs. Cauldwell led the other. It was a piece by Martin Shaw called "Song of the Music Maker." Florence eagerly watched to see if Arthur was carrying the card with the introduction on it. She saw him to her left, and he was completely focused on the task at hand. No notes were visible.

It was a lovely beginning to the concert. Each subsequent song was introduced by one or two choristers. Ms. Moster and Mrs. Cauldwell simply stepped aside and let the children take the microphone. It seemed to make the audience more attentive too. It was clear that the speakers had rehearsed what they had to say.

When it came time for Arthur to introduce "Adiemus", Florence realized that her hands were clammy. Arthur took the card out of his pants pocket as he walked up to the microphone. Florence was astonished to see that he didn't seem nervous at all.

"Good evening, Ladies and Gentlemen," he began. "Tonight you are going to hear a song called 'Adiemus.'" Arthur cleared his throat, looked down at his card, and continued. "It is by the composer Karl Jenkins. Do not try to understand the words: they are all nonsense." He smiled at the audience, and some people laughed. "This is what the composer wanted. Just listen to the music." Arthur smiled again, put his notes in his pocket, and walked back to the choir.

Florence smiled from ear to ear. She was stunned by Arthur's composure. He didn't have a loud confidence—just a simple, straight forward, honest presence. She could see that Bucket was beaming in the back row of the soprano section. Florence quietly took a pen out of her purse and wrote Arthur's name as speaker under the Jenkins song in the program. She kept a collection of everything the children had done over the years. She wanted to make sure that this moment wasn't forgotten. Florence looked up again and saw that the choir was really enjoying this piece. She closed her eyes and let the music flow over her.

Before the last number of the evening, Mrs. Cauldwell finally took the microphone.

"Ladies and Gentlemen, thank you so much for coming this evening. Thanks especially to Ms. Moster for her leadership tonight." On cue, a chorister from the Junior Children's Choir came out with a giant bouquet for the conductor. Then Ms. Moster thanked Mrs. Cauldwell. She also had Diane Black come forward and receive a bouquet for her year as managing director of the choirs. Finally, Mrs. Black took over.

"I know you think we've forgotten someone. Well, we haven't. Mr. Biggs, will you please come forward?" Mrs. Black gestured for Carey to join her at the front of the stage.

"Some of you may not know that this was Mr. Biggs' very last concert with the Moorland Children's Choir. Tonight we are thanking him for his years of music-making with all of our choirs. Thank you so much, Carey!" The audience rose as one, clapping furiously. From the back of the auditorium, Florence could see Bucket and Providence carrying what looked like a brass music stand. The crowd continued clapping while the girls handed over the gift and took turns hugging Mr. Biggs.

"Excuse me," said Mr. Biggs. Everyone sat down, expecting the piano player to say his farewells. "I am deeply touched. It has been a lot of fun to tickle the ivories with these folks. I will miss them. Thank you one and all," he said, almost breaking down. He bowed and made his way to the piano.

"One last note," said Mrs. Black. "I am giving all of you one week's grace to have in your tour forms. That's my absolute, final cut-off date—one week from today!"

Florence barely heard the last number. She had yet to tell Arthur and Bucket that they were moving to Tirovica in August. Bucket had been asking her almost every day if she had signed the form. She didn't want to disappoint her daughter, but she reasoned that there would surely be other tours in her future. Arthur was too young to go on the tour, so it wasn't an issue with him, thankfully. Besides, Florence thought, they would be back in a year and could join the Moorland Children's Choir again. Yes, it would all work out...she hoped.

Chapter Thirty-Three

More News!

After the concert, Florence congratulated her children on all of their hard work and a successful concert. To celebrate, she took Bucket and Arthur to a little ice cream shop called Two Bears not far from their home. It was an old corner store that had been converted into a teddy-bear-making workshop with an ice cream parlour on the side. Arthur ordered the usual—bubblegum. Bucket and Florence both got tiger-tiger. The evening was still warm even though the sun was low on the horizon. Last year they had walked all the way from their house to the ice cream shop with Presto.

"Remember when we brought Presto with us?" their mother asked.

"Yeah, I do," Arthur laughed. "My bubblegum ice cream landed on the sidewalk."

"And Presto snapped it up and scarfed it down!" finished Bucket.

"She got sick, didn't she, mom?" Arthur asked.

"She certainly did. But I'm sure she'd eat another if she were given the chance." The three of them sat down on a bench facing the sun.

"It feels like summer already!" Bucket said. "I can't believe the musical is next week!"

"That reminds me," her mother said. "I have to finish the sashes for the girl's chorus this week-end. I think they'll be really pretty."

"I like the policemen. They have neat uniforms and their batons are really funny," Arthur said, who had yet to miss a rehearsal.

"I am really looking forward to the performance, Bucket," Florence stated.

"I'm getting excited too," Bucket admitted. "You know, it's kind of neat having Ms. Moster helping out so much. Oh, she asked me tonight to remind you to get in that tour form, mom."

They had almost finished their ice cream cones. Florence thought that this might be a good time to give them the news.

"Bucket, Arthur, I have something exciting to tell you. You know that I have a sabbatical next year," she said, stalling.

"Of course we know," Bucket said.

"Yeah, you wanna be a student," Arthur added, rolling his eyes.

"That's true. I do. And the best thing about next year is that I've been accepted to study at the University of Tirovica! We're going to be moving to the island," she ended triumphantly, hoping her enthusiasm would transmit itself to her children.

"Is that far away?" Arthur asked, who had been there when he was only eleven months old.

"It will be probably a two-day drive. On the way there, we get to go through the mountains. And then we have to take a ferry to get to Tirovica."

"Isn't that where Grandpa Dunne lives?" Bucket asked.

"Yes it is. We might get to see him and nana Judy," she said. Her father had re-married after her mother's death to an English cousin of her mother's family. On paper it should have been a wonderful solution to her father's loneliness. Her father was completely occupied with all things Judy now. It could be that her father was deliriously happy with his marriage, but the family wouldn't know because his appearance in their lives was a rarity.

"What about school, mom?" Bucket asked, now starting to frown.

"I will spend some time in July, when you're with your father at the lake, to go to Tirovica and investigate."

"What about dad?" Arthur asked, now starting to look as worried as Bucket.

"Of course I've talked this over with your dad before I'd even consider moving away from Moorland. Remember, kids, it's only for a year. He is agreeable. We'll be back for part of the Christmas holidays too. I'm sure he'll phone and write as well."

"Does this mean I won't be going on the choir tour?" Bucket wondered, starting to sound truly concerned.

"It does, Bucket. But I'm sure there will be oodles of opportunities where we're going," assured her Mother. Both her children looked shell-shocked. The sun was starting to set, and a cool breeze softly blew down the adjoining street to the little ice cream store. They quietly piled into the car and drove home. There was no conversation.

As the children got ready for bed that night, Florence wondered if she was doing the right thing for her family. She went into Arthur's bedroom and saw that he was writing and drawing in his sketchbook, but he put it away as soon as he saw her come through the door. She sat on the edge of the bed and pulled the covers up around his shoulders.

"Mom, isn't the island where they have earthquakes?" he asked, wide-eyed.

"It's true—sometimes they have tremors. But they haven't had a really strong earthquake for a long, long, long time," she assured him.

"What will we do with Presto? She doesn't like long trips," Arthur informed her.

"Hmmm. That's a good question. Maybe we can come up with a solution for that together," his mother said as she bent down and kissed him.

She found Presto in Bucket's room. It was unusual for the dog not to be on Arthur's bed first. And then Florence noticed why—Bucket was crying.

"What's wrong?" her mother asked as she sat down on the bed beside the dog.

"Mom, you said you would think about the tour. Ro and Pro are both going," she wailed and continued to cry into Presto's dark fur.

"Yes, I said that, didn't I?" her mother admitted. "I am really sorry that you won't be going. I know it will be hard to be away from your friends. Don't forget Mommy has friends too that she will really miss."

"I bet you told everybody we're leaving," Bucket sobbed.

"Let me see, I told your dad and aunt Edie. So far that's it."

"Really?" Bucket started wiping the tears from her eyes.

"Yes, really." Florence smoothed the wet, tangled hair out of Bucket's eyes and gave her a kiss on the forehead. "I have a feeling that you'll really like Tirovica. I know it will be a big change, Bucket, but it will be for all of us. We'll be in it together."

"I guess you're right, mom," Bucket sighed and slumped into her mother's arms.

"It will work out—you'll see."

"There's one more thing Mom," Bucket said shyly.

"What's that sweetheart?"

"I might have to kiss Donald."

"You mean, you might have to kiss Frederick," Florence said, amused. "You are acting the part of Mabel, and he is acting the part of Frederick. I'm sure Mrs. Cauldwell doesn't want you to do anything inappropriate. It's just a kiss on the cheek, isn't it?"

"Yes, but it's so embarrassing!"

"Did you ever think that he might be feeling the same way?"

"I guess so. Maybe he gets teased too!" Bucket realized.

"I'm sure he does. And remember, the kiss will only be a very, very small part of the whole musical. Everyone is there to see the singing, acting and dancing...the whole show. Having said that, I can still appreciate how you must feel, Bucket."

"Promise you won't laugh at me," she pleaded.

"I would not do anything of the sort, Brigitte Ethel Boisvert. You are my shining light!" Florence gave her another kiss good night, petted the dog, and turned out the bedside lamp as she left the room.

Later that night, when she sat down at her sewing machine to work on the satin sashes, Florence mulled over the conversations she'd had with Arthur and Bucket. There would be more questions in the future, she was certain. But on the whole, she felt that they were not taking the news of their impending move with a huge amount of negativity. Perhaps it was because it was just for a year and they would be returning to their own home. The question of what to do with Presto was one that Florence had not seriously considered. It would have to be put on the lengthy to-do list along with renting their home, packing, moving, finding digs in Tirovica, locating a school for Bucket and Arthur, opening up a new bank account, counting her pennies...Florence sighed—one day at a time.

Chapter Thirty-Four

The Pirates of Penzance

THE NEXT WEEK WAS FILLED WITH REHEARSALS for the musical with all the props and set pieces in use. Excitement was building. The venue for the performance was the theatre of the local Moorland High School, which held about three hundred people—smaller than the auditorium that was used for the choral recitals at the university. This made it the perfect size for Bannister Elementary School's small community. By the second week of June, all of the high school classes were finished, and the students were slated to write exams starting the week after the musical. The high school drama teacher had been a former student of Mrs. Cauldwell's, which was the only reason they were able to use the performance space. High school drama departments in Moorland jealously guarded their theatre spaces, even though these stages were commonly not in use for certain times of the year.

The day of the performance was the first day the children would be using the space, since they were allowed to be in the theatre and backstage area only for the afternoon and evening. Mrs. Cauldwell, Ms. Moster, and the high school drama teacher had the schedule tightly co-ordinated to allow for a complete run-through of the show. Miss Mitchell was going to be backstage for the performance, helping out with costumes and cues. Two students from the high school ran the lights, although they were set for the previous show of *Les Miserables.* That would have to suffice.

Bucket came home after school filled with stories of how exciting it was to be on a proper stage. Arthur listened to everything and reminded his mother to look for the Jolly Rogers. Florence counted up all the tickets she was going to bring to the theatre. She and Arthur had their own tickets; plus she was meeting Jan and Dorothy at the high school with theirs. She had already given Jean and Marie their tickets. Florence knew there would be a line-up of parents waiting to get in, so she was preparing to be there in good time to make sure everyone had a decent seat.

As she predicted, other parents who had dropped off their children early were automatically starting to form a line. She did likewise and asked Arthur to go to the foyer of the school to be on the look-out for their friends. Just as the doors were opened to the theatre, Arthur arrived with Jan and Dorothy in tow. Everyone was all smiles anticipating the event. As they slowly walked forward in the long line, Arthur nudged her.

"Mom, I saw dad and Marie," he said.

"Run back and tell them I'll save some seats," his mother suggested. Off he went, returning just as they rounded the corner into the theatre itself. They managed to find six seats fairly close together in the audience on the right side. Jean and Marie finally appeared and settled themselves just behind Jan and Dorothy. Introductions were made all around because Dorothy and Jan had yet to meet Jean's new wife.

"Are you excited about moving to the island?" asked Dorothy, bending over to talk to Arthur.

"I guess so," he replied. "I'm not sure what to do with Presto. She doesn't like to travel."

"I don't think any dog would like to travel a great distance," Jan agreed.

"I see by the program that you had something to do with the sets," Jean said, leaning into the conversation.

"You must have heard from Arthur that he did quite a bit of the artwork,"Jan responded, looking at Arthur with a smile. By now the seats were almost full, and there was a general buzz in the audience. Marie touched Jean's arm and pulled him back.

"How long will the performance be?" she whispered to Jean. Florence turned around in her seat to address Marie.

"It's the junior version of the operetta, so it should be under an hour."

"It's the first time we've had a sitter, and I didn't want it to be for too long," she said anxiously.

"Don't worry, Marie," Jean said, just as the house lights went down.

The stage lights came up on the rocks of the sea shore and the painted backdrop. A hush spread over the crowd. The overture began. At a break in the music, from the back of the theatre came a spine-tingling sound.

"Aargh! Pieces of eight! Avast, ye swabs!" cried twelve different voices. The pirates appeared, moving down the aisles toward the stage. They waved their Jolly Rogers while yelling their pirate doggerel. It was a thrilling, attention-grabbing beginning to the musical. Arthur grabbed his mother's hand in excitement and pointed to one of the flags going by.

"That one's mine," Arthur whispered. She squeezed his hand wordlessly and gave him a big smile.

The pirates looked like they were enjoying their roles. They did a good job of passing around the jug of "rum" and held their tankards high in song. The pianist, Ms. Moster's mother, was doing a commendable job of accompanying the students with just the right amount of volume. Mrs. Cauldwell conducted from a stool below the stage so that the attention would be on the performers.

Mr. Harbicht's "rocks" seemed to be holding up well. The pirates alternately sat and stood on them. Donald, who was playing Frederick, looked an appealing character in his sailor outfit. He had a clear, unwavering voice. The nursemaid character, Ruth, stood out for her strong singing and sense of comic timing. Florence thought that it was one of the most difficult roles to ask a young girl to play because Ruth was always referred to as old and not very pretty in the script. When the pirate king had his turn, he used the entire stage during his solo, moving around, and on top of the set pieces as he sang. He waved one of the Jolly Rogers in a wide sweeping arc, commanding his team of cutthroats as the whole group moved off-stage.

When the girl's chorus came on, Florence squeezed Arthur's hand and mouthed the words, "Bucket's turn" to him. Providence had her long hair curled in ringlets and preceded Bucket coming on stage. The white and pink satin sashes gave some uniformity to the frilly party dresses that they were wearing. As a chorus, the girls were in perfect unison, even though they were moving among the rocks as they sang. The acoustics were very good in the theatre, making it possible for the audience to hear the individual spoken lines. It was a vast improvement on the school's gymnasium.

Frederick's appearance elicited a suitably shocked response from the entire chorus of girls. And then Bucket, who had been standing beside Providence in the group of girls, stepped out to centre stage in her role as Mabel.

"Oh, sisters, have you no pity? Shame! Shame!" Bucket said with commanding authority. But it was her singing—a sweet, high soprano—that took Florence's breath away. She looked down at Arthur. He looked at her and mouthed, "Wow!" She glanced over to Jan and Dorothy but they were completely focused on the performance. When Bucket launched into her solo, Florence caught herself holding her breath. Her daughter soared up to the highest notes effortlessly. It was a magical moment. The audience erupted into spontaneous applause at the final notes of the song.

After the comic confrontation between the girls and the pirates, Rowena came on as the major general. The timing for this song was crucial. Rowena was relishing her part, making her character self-important and bombastic, just the way he should be. She spit out all the words to her difficult solo with panache. At the end, she doffed her huge hat and made a bow, to the audience's approval.

The finale for act one was a joyous rendition; with twenty-four students singing, it filled the auditorium. Then the lights went down on the backstage area while Frederick and Ruth acted their scene on the stage apron. The girl's chorus had already exited because they had to change out of their summer dresses and into their Victorian style nightgowns. Mr. Harbicht and Miss Mitchell, both dressed all in black, rolled down the night-time scenery for act two. While they were thus engaged, Ms. Moster came out to turn all of the rocks around 180 degrees revealing the stones of the chapel ruin. By the time the scene between Ruth and Frederick was over, the backdrop changers had left, but Ms. Moster was not quite done turning the rocks around.

The accompanist quickly began to play the introductory bars for act two, which gave just enough time for the rock turner to finish and the major general with his bevy of girls to enter. Each of the girls wore a white night cap. Along with their white nightgowns it was a stark contrast to the darkness of the night-time set. Rowena was wearing a thick, white-and-red striped flannelette nightgown with red-and-gold epaulettes and a red night cap. With the major general centre stage sitting on the tallest stone and the girls grouped aesthetically around "him," it was quite a sight.

After the sad and sorrowful tune that introduced act two, everyone was surprised by the entrance of the policeman's chorus right through the audience. With their dark uniforms, oversized truncheons, helmets and gold badges that were all made by the art club, they created an impressive sight. The strong beat of the song and the underlying "Ta-ran-ta-ra" that wove its way throughout the melody made for a grand display of marching manoeuvres. Florence thought it was especially funny to see Bucket, as Mabel, in her white nightgown conducting them around the stage.

The following scenes were extremely well acted and sung. Florence kept marvelling at the level of performance of such a young group of people. She knew that children were quite often capable of much more than adults gave them credit for. She also knew that some of the worst offenders were teachers who pigeon-holed students just from looking at their files without even meeting the child. Mrs. Cauldwell had all of the students in grades five and six involved in this production. There was not a student left out of any chorus. So far nobody had forgotten their lines. And if some of the singing wasn't pitch-perfect, it was sung with conviction.

The final altercation between the policemen and the pirates was well choreographed and done in slow motion, in time to the music. Now the pirates got to use their swords and the policemen, their truncheons. It would have taken many rehearsals to get the timing just right. The fact that they were singing at the same time was remarkable.

The ensuing scenes, complex in language nuance with "orphan" and "often" being the highlight, seemed to go by all too quickly. The girl's chorus enjoyed their unison crying of "Oh! Rapture!" when their moment came. Donald gave Bucket a brief, chaste kiss on the cheek after the last song. With the policemen, pirates and girls all on stage, the finale to the musical lived up to its name. The girl's chorus curtsied, followed by the policeman's salute. The pirate chorus leapt to the front, brandishing their swords and shouting, "Argh!" Finally the principal characters joined hands and came forward.

By now the audience was on its feet, clapping with the enthusiasm that only a crowd of parents, friends, and relatives can bring. Florence felt tears course down her cheeks that, try as she might, she could not hold back. She was so happy for Bucket and for the children and teachers involved. From her own theatre experiences, she realized that this was an incredible achievement for everyone.

"Are you OK, mom?" Arthur asked, a bit concerned.

"Sure I'm OK," she said. "I'm just really happy and proud!"

"Me too," agreed Arthur. "This was the best!"

With the audience still on its feet, Mrs. Cauldwell and her team of teachers came out to accept big bouquets of red roses. They thanked everyone concerned, especially the parents who had supported the huge endeavour from the beginning.

After the clapping had died down and the children and teachers had left the stage, the audience made its slow way out of the theatre and into the hallway and foyer of the high school.

"That was quite something!" Dorothy said, articulating what they all felt.

"Wasn't your sister great?" Jean said, ruffling Arthur's hair affectionately.

"She was awesome!" enthused Arthur.

"Those backdrops added so much to the show," Florence commented.

"Yeah, that was pretty cool how they changed from one act to the other so quickly," Marie added, who had stopped looking at her watch early on in the performance.

"I think that was Jan's brainchild," Florence offered as they found their way to the foyer.

"It was fun painting it!" Arthur said. "And we get to keep our pirate flags!"

By now they had reached the large foyer of the school. People were milling about, looking for cast members coming out of the green rooms. Bit by bit they appeared. Shouts of congratulation greeted each new arrival. Other members of the Bannister Elementary School were heading out of the building with arms of costumes or set pieces to be loaded into the teacher's waiting vans and trucks.

Finally Bucket appeared. She spied her father first and leapt into his arms.

"You were wonderful my girl," he said, giving her a giant hug. Marie came next with a big hug as well.

"I'm so proud of you Bucket," he said as he put her down. "We have to go right now to pick up the sitter. But we'll see you soon."

"Sure, dad. I'm just glad you could come," Bucket said all smiles, and waved to them as they left. Just as she turned around to give her attention to everyone else, Arthur grabbed her and gave her a big hug. Florence laughed.

"Hey, bro, did you like it?" Bucket asked.

"No way, it was terrible, sis! Yeuch!" Arthur said, laughing and giving her a playful punch.

"Wow, I didn't know you were coming, Jan and Dorothy!" Bucket exclaimed.

"We wouldn't have missed it for the world," Dorothy said, giving Bucket a warm embrace.

"My turn!" Jan added, enveloping Bucket in a bear hug.

"Everybody loved the art-work., Jan," Bucket said. Finally Florence gathered up Bucket and twirled her around.

"Poor wandering one!" she teased. "Are you ready to come home yet?"

"Oh, Mom, it was so much fun!!" Bucket laughed, turned, and curtsied to them all.

"I'd like to get some pictures by the marquee before everyone leaves," Dorothy said. Miss Mitchell's class had made a huge poster that showed photographs of each of the students in costume. It was displayed on one of the walls of the foyer, making it a perfect photo opportunity. Dorothy organized different groupings until all the possibilities were exhausted. Finally they made their way to their vehicles and wished each other a good night.

Chapter Thirty-Five

Looking Forward

AT HOME, LATER THAT EVENING, Florence looked in on Bucket. She had fallen asleep quickly, the result of a long day. It had started out with school in the morning followed by rehearsals all afternoon. She had just had time for a quick bite to eat before arriving at the theatre in the early evening. Florence realized that her daughter put 110 percent into everything she did. Watching her lie there so peacefully, Florence marvelled again at the force of life that was Bucket.

At the doorway to her son's room, Florence contemplated Presto and Arthur fast asleep. As she thought about the last week of school coming up, she prayed that it was going to be a peaceful one for Arthur. Jean had told her that the phone call with Greg's father had not been very comfortable at all. He had been remarkably lukewarm to any discussion of his son's behaviour. She guessed that there was probably some denial going on. At least Henry had changed his conduct. Arthur had attended his birthday party, with some gentle persuasion on her part. It seemed to have set a positive tone for the succeeding weeks at school.

His sketchbook, as usual was on his bedside table. She hesitated, but ended up taking it with her to the living room. Curling up in her grandfather's old rocker she opened the book and looked at Arthur's last sketch. It was a pencil drawing of Presto lying on Arthur's bed, much as she looked tonight. It wasn't in exactly correct proportions, but he had somehow captured the dog's hairy smiling mouth and questioning eyebrows. Above and underneath the drawing, Florence read a poem in Arthur's sprawling printing style.

Dog
My friend
You listen to me
A secret
A cry
You laugh when I laugh
You run fast

She closed the book and held it to her chest, pondering just what she was doing by ripping her children away from all that they loved and held dear. It would be impossible to take Presto with them. Florence knew that the dog's absence would be really hard on Bucket and Arthur. That was yet another thing they had to discuss as a family. She still had a few weeks before the children went with their father to his family cottage at a distant Saskatchewan lake. Florence hoped that there would be enough time before Arthur and Bucket went on holidays to work through all of the issues that were uppermost in her mind.

She wondered once again if this wasn't a terribly selfish act. All along Florence thought she had the needs of her children at the forefront of her life. The enormity of the move and what it meant for all of them was starting to dawn on her. Florence had been utterly preoccupied with day-to-day living—her work, Arthur's terrible situation, the school musical—that she had shelved those very real concerns to the proverbial back burner.

Florence silenced the negative voice in her brain. Her children were at the perfect age for an adventure. She felt certain that the island would entrance them as much as it had captivated her in the past. Only time would tell. She wondered how they would all feel next June, contemplating their final few weeks in Tirovica. Deep down Florence believed that the year away would be worth all the effort that a move would take.

Chapter Thirty-Six

Last Day of School

AT LUNCH RECESS, WORD GOT OUT that Arthur was leaving the school next year. Seymour, Lau, Addison, and Lance were just walking around the schoolyard in the sun, all their games forgotten.

"I wish I was going with you, Arthur," Addison said. "They play a lot of soccer on the island. And sometimes a team gets to take a ferry."

"That would be fun, taking a ferry," enthused Seymour.

"I've been there," Lance boasted. "The best thing is going on a Zodiac. You can make big waves with that thing!"

"What's a Zodiac?" Arthur asked, who was still uncertain about the move. He was sure he'd miss his buddies. At least he was going to be able to play with them after school today at Lance's house.

"It's like a turbo-charged rubber dingy," he explained. "You should see the motor—it's huge!"

"The whales," Lau said in a soft voice. "Go see the whales."

"Yeah, my mom's talked about them," Arthur admitted.

"You're so lucky," Seymour said. "We'll just be here doing the same boring stuff, just like this year."

"Except when we got to do pirates," Addison reminded them.

"Argh!" yelled Lance, brandishing an imaginary sword. Pretty soon all of the boys were yelling their piratical yells and leaping about. They continued jumping and sword fighting until they came to a clump of trees at the end of the playground.

"Get lost, you losers!!" Greg screamed. He was leading a group of grade two students in some kind of spying game. They were crouched down in the underbrush but came out when Arthur and the other boys drew near.

"Argh!" they shouted in response.

"You are so stupid," Greg continued, but not coming any closer to the group.

"Look who's talkin'," Lance challenged.

"Heard yer leavin', rat face," sneered Greg, pointing to Arthur and ignoring Lance. The younger boys started a chorus of "Rat face, rat face, rat face," with Greg's encouragement.

But Arthur just looked at Greg, deciding that if his pal Henry wasn't with him, he had nothing to fear even if the name-calling made him feel a little sick.

"When are you gonna grow up, Greg?" Addison asked. "Looks like you failed, 'cause all your buddies are in grade two."

"Why you dirty dog!" Greg screamed as he started after Addison, who was well aware the effect the taunt would have on him. Soon all of the grade two boys were trailing after Greg as he tried to catch Addison. Lance and the others laughed as they watched the soccer player weave around the goal posts and thread his way in and out of the playground equipment. Greg's group couldn't keep up and started to fall by the wayside. Then the bell rang. Arthur caught up to Addison as they formed their lines to go into the school.

"You sure got him going!" Arthur said in appreciation.

"Yeah, well, the last recess of the year. Ya gotta have some excitement!" Addison said, and both boys laughed. Greg had gathered up his group by now, but he wasn't allowed to go into the grade two line with them. He was trying to get them to repeat the chant. Finally he gave up and had to go to the end of grade three.

After lunch there was a talent show in Bucket's classroom. It was how Mr. Harbicht's grade fives always ended the school year. Students were allowed to go solo or perform something with a partner or a small group. Sometimes he let them do both if he thought the pieces were adequately prepared. No parents were allowed; it was a student event only.

Desks were moved into a double semi-circle to create a space big enough at the front of the room to accommodate the larger group. For the afternoon, Mr. Harbicht had moved in the school's piano. All the desks were cleaned off and the boards were too. Their teacher had put a large Happy Holidays sign tacked up at the front of the room. Everything else was cleaned up and neatened up. His vast library of books were straightened and dusted. Mr. Harbicht would be returning to Bannister Elementary to teach another grade five class in September.

Bucket was excited. She was going to be part of a dance number that Rowena had thought up along with Providence and Chim. They had been practising on the weekends ever since *The Pirates of Penzance* had finished. She was happy because it gave her extra time with her chums. And after school, she would be going over to Providence's house. She was anxious that she would not be seeing her friends for a long, long time. In July she and Arthur would be with their dad and in August they would be moving. She tried to push that thought from her mind as everyone got ready for the afternoon's entertainment.

The whole afternoon went by so quickly. Mr. Harbicht kept an eagle eye on the time to make sure nobody lost an opportunity to show what they had rehearsed. Some students played the piano, either solos or duets. Some sang songs or read stories that they had written. Donald, who had played Frederick in the musical, did a comedy routine with a series of knock-knock jokes. Two of the girls recited a really long poem called, "Jabberwocky," each saying every other verse. Bucket thought it was the craziest thing she had ever heard. She could hardly wait to tell her mother and Arthur about it.

Finally Bucket's group got up to perform. They were a little nervous going up in front of their classmates, but Rowena had designed the dance so that they started out with their backs to the audience. They didn't have as much room as they had rehearsed in, so they would have to be careful. It seemed like the music would never start. A few of the students in the class started to titter, but they finally heard the opening bars and began the routine. Once she saw Providence smile as they performed their first turn, Bucket stopped worrying. Chim bumped a desk towards the end, but not enough to really affect the rhythm, so they ignored it and kept on going. The girls held their final pose at the end of the music while their classmates applauded.

"Thank you so much, ladies," Mr. Harbicht said. "I would like to thank everyone for putting on a wonderful celebration this afternoon. Please give each other a round of applause." As was customary in his grade five class, the students clapped loudly on their desks.

"I'd also like to thank you for your hard work this year. Good luck to all of you next year. To those of you who I will not be seeing in the hallowed halls of Bannister Elementary, happy trails," he said, glancing in Bucket's direction. The bell rang. The children cheered, and Mr. Harbicht gave them a big smile.

Chapter Thirty-Seven

Good-bye Moorland

SUMMER CAME AND WENT ON A HOT WIND as it has a habit of doing sometimes. Bucket and Arthur spent the month of July with their father, Marie and baby Genevieve at the family cottage. They swam, carried water from the pump, fed the baby, got bitten by mosquitoes, and generally had a wonderful time. Florence meanwhile was completely occupied with renting the house and the overall logistics of the move.

Her sister, Edie, had arrived in the first part of July to help her select the right renters. Florence had put an ad in the paper the previous week and had come up with a final list of three families. Edie was proficient in human resources so she was an invaluable asset. After all of the prospective renters had been interviewed, it looked like there was a front runner. The one difficulty was that they wanted the home one week before Florence had planned to go to the island. Edie convinced her that they were the best candidates anyway because they had a three-year-old daughter, and the father was going to the college six blocks away. Florence had the family sign a rental agreement. That was one more item ticked off her list.

Florence left the second last week of the month on a trip to the island. She took a few things that she knew she would need to store in the meantime at her father's home. He and his wife would not be there. They liked to spend as much time as possible travelling. This was fine with Florence because it gave her uninterrupted time to find rental accommodation and a school for the children.

By the time the last week of July rolled around, Florence had already found a two bedroom apartment in the basement of a hundred-year-old house in Tirovica. She had enrolled the children in a school that was just four blocks away. She searched out a local bank and opened an account, which she would need for her school board sabbatical payments. She even found the time to tour the university, making sure graduate studies had her on their roster.

Back in Moorland, August was a blur of deciding what to keep and what to take. She and the children only had two weeks to make all of the decisions that would impact them the coming year. Florence decided that they could do without their television. This caused quite a bit of discussion, but in the end they all agreed.

After washing, organizing, and packing, Florence had twenty small containers that she sent by bus to their new address in Tirovica. The rest of what they owned was boxed and moved into the bedroom in the downstairs basement. Finally the time came when their Moorland home was scrubbed to the rafters. The grass was mowed and the giant hedge was clipped. They were ready.

Jan and Dorothy Clayton offered to take the family prior to their leaving for Tirovica. They were to stay with them overnight before heading out on their trek through the mountains. Florence's feeling of being overwhelmed by the exertions of the summer eased a bit as she and the children sat outside with the two sisters on their front porch. From where they were sitting, Moorland looked like a toy town in the distance. The evening was unusually hot and humid. Presto and Whiskey were lying at their feet, momentarily quiet.

"I wonder where you'll be this time tomorrow night?" Dorothy pondered.

"Somewhere in the mountains," replied Florence. "Thanks for taking us in. And thanks cannot even begin to express how grateful we are to you for adopting Presto for this coming year."

"Actually, we noticed how well she gets along with Whiskey," commented Jan. "They are good companions."

"Why don't you take the dogs down to the fox house with the kids, Flo?" Dorothy suggested. Arthur and Bucket seemed too subdued for her liking.

"What a good idea," Florence said. "We need to stretch our legs before that long drive tomorrow."

Both dogs and the children seemed reluctant to move, but Florence pulled them along with her eagerness.

"Mom, do I look like a rat face?" Arthur asked quietly as they walked on the trail down to the overlook. Bucket and the dogs were out of earshot ahead of them.

"Absolutely not, my handsome young man!" she exclaimed. "Whatever made you think that?"

"No reason," he said. He put his hand in hers. "Will I like Tirovica?"

"I am betting on it!" His mother smiled. They caught up to Bucket and the dogs. She was sitting on the garden swing beside the fox house. The dogs lay down on a patch of prairie grass just in front of her. Arthur sat down next to Bucket. Their mother stood beside them, looking out at Arrow River which stretched before them.

"Bucket, you're really quiet tonight," her mother observed.

"Don't you know she's sad!" Arthur said.

"It's OK to be sad. I'm sad. I'll miss Dorothy and Jan."

"I'll miss dad and Marie and the baby," Arthur added.

"I'm going to miss Ro and Pro!" blurted Bucket.

"I'll miss Presto sooooooo much," Arthur intoned.

"Shhh. Look over there kids," whispered their mother as she quietly moved to sit beside the two dogs. She pointed to the other side of the fox house, to the crest of a hill a little ways away. There, on the very top, stood a lone coyote. It was gazing out at the river and then turned and seemed to look at them.

"Yip yip yippee," it howled, echoed by the pack a moment later. The family froze. Florence held onto the dogs, fearing they might give chase. They too were transfixed. A moment later the coyote disappeared into the brush, the pack remaining invisible.

"I think it was saying good-bye," Bucket said.

"You might be right," her mother responded, smiling.

The family stayed on the hill for a while, bathed in the colours of the setting sun.

As Inspired!

This is a bonus page for a curious reader. There's music in Moorland and here are some videos to give you an idea of what Arthur and Bucket were singing. Enjoy!

Chapter Two	"Streets of London" by Ralph McTell YouTube: Cluster Voices, "Streets of London"
Chapter Seventeen	"Sakura" (in Japanese) arranged by Shin-Ichiro Yokoyama YouTube: Treble Choir, "Sakura" "Margery Maketh the Tea" by W. H. Anderson YouTube: "Margery Make the Tea", Steve Murray (Harmonia Choir of Ottawa) "N'Kosi Sikelel' iAfrika" by Enoch Mankayi Sontonga YouTube: Cantare Children's Choir Sings South Africa's National Anthem
Chapter Thirty-Two	"Adiemus" by Karl Jenkins YouTube: "Adiemus" (Karl Jenkins) Singapore Symphony Children's Choir
Chapter Thirty-Four	"Poor Wandering One" from Pirates of Penzance by Gilbert and Sullivan YouTube: Nicole (age 13) sings "Poor Wandering One" from Pirates

Bullying

Arthur and his friends were subject to bullying by their classmates. In the early 1990s there weren't many resources for dealing with this frightening situation. Today, social media adds yet another dimension. However, there are more supports for children and families in need. If any of my readers are suffering or know of others who are, please access the following helpful links:

- **Kids Help Phone** (kidshelpphone.ca) is free, confidential, and a multi-lingual support.
- **School Resource Officer** (SRO), if your school has one, is set up to deal with this kind of situation.
- **www.BullyingCanada.ca** is set up similar to the Kids Help Phone.
- **www.Prevnet.ca** is for teens and their unique needs.

Acknowledgements

I'd like to thank Michael Pietrobon, from Foglio Custom Book Specialists, for his encouragement in publishing *The Adventures of Bucket and Arthur* as a series. Thanks also to the Airdrie writer's group and Kelly Kirkpatrick-Lauzon for starting me out on my NaNoWriMo adventures. A big debt of gratitude goes to my husband, Rick, who challenged me to get off the rickety fence of indecision!

About the Author

Born in Saskatchewan, Sheila Humphrey lives in the foothills of Alberta where she writes, paints and sings. Her poetry and prose appear in the annual magazine, *Voice and Vision* (2016 - 2025). Her writing also appears in the following anthologies: *Prairie Stories—Contest Submissions from Jake and the Kid*, edited by Rebecca Wohlgemuth, Rosebud Theatre, Rosebud, Alberta. 2011; *The Short and Sweet of it*, edited by Susan Cheeves King, Grace Publishing, Broken Arrow, OK. 2018; *Flowers of Remembrance*, by Tandy Balson and Friends, Eildon Hills Publishing. 2024.

www.ingramcontent.com/pod-product-compliance
Lightning Source LLC
Jackson TN
JSHW020854140126
96898JS00001B/112
9781069813008